BOOKS BY

JOHN SWARTZWELDER

THE TIME MACHINE DID IT (2004)

DOUBLE WONDERFUL (2005)

HOW I CONQUERED YOUR PLANET (2006)

THE EXPLODING DETECTIVE (2007)

DEAD MEN SCARE ME STUPID (2008)

EARTH VS. EVERYBODY (2009)

THE LAST DETECTIVE ALIVE (2010)

THE FIFTY FOOT DETECTIVE (2011)

THE FIFTY FOOT DETECTIVE

JOHN SWARTZWELDER

Kennydale Books
Chatsworth, California

Copyright © 2011
by John Swartzwelder

Published by:
Kennydale Books
P.O. Box 3925
Chatsworth, California 91313-3925

All Rights Reserved. No part of this book may be reproduced or transmitted in any form or by any means, electronic or mechanical, including photocopying, recording or by any information storage and retrieval system, without written permission from the author, except for the inclusion of brief quotations in a review.

First Printing March, 2011

ISBN 13 (paperback edition) 978-0-9822736-4-7
ISBN 13 (hardback edition) 978-0-9822736-5-4
ISBN 10 (paperback edition) 0-9822736-4-9
ISBN 10 (hardback edition) 0-9822736-5-7

Library of Congress Control Number: 2011902448

This book is a work of fiction. Names, characters, places and incidents either are the product of the author's imagination or are used fictitiously, and any resemblance to actual persons, living or dead, events, or locales is entirely coincidental.

Printed in the United States of America

CHAPTER ONE

"You're taking the fall."
"But I'm the judge."
"You're going down."
"Bailiff! Seize this man!"
"Bailiff! Seize the judge!"

The courtroom was thrown into an uproar by this sudden and dramatic turn of events. There was confusion everywhere, especially in the mind of the bailiff. He wasn't sure what to do. On the one hand, he was an officer of the court, so he should probably do his job. On the other hand, he had just received a direct order from Lucius B. "Loose" Cannon, Private Eye, the toughest, rudest, most successful private investigator in the annals of crime prevention. And he knew that people defied orders from Loose Cannon at their peril. Prison cells and hospitals from one end of the country to the other were filled with people who had defied him. Dentist's offices, too. And those hair restoration places.

2

"Did you hear me, bailiff?" demanded the judge.

The bailiff still hesitated. He didn't like either one of his options. He wondered if it was too late to call in sick. He figured it probably was. But then he realized that the judge's question had given him an opening—a way to buy some time by pretending that, in fact, he couldn't hear. He explained to the increasingly impatient court that when he was a child, see, his family had had to sell one of his ears to buy food, and later on, when the horse died and the new wide screen TVs came out, the other ear had to go. And the ears he'd ordered from that mail order ear house in Earville had been stolen by the Ear Gang, so... but it was all turning into too long of a story, and was getting more unbelievable all the time. And everyone could see his ears anyway. They were the size of dinner plates. And they were getting redder by the minute, the more he lied about them.

"Bailiff! Stop making excuses and seize that man, or I'll have somebody seize you!"

This decided the bailiff. He pulled out his gun and apprehensively approached Loose Cannon, who was watching him with narrowed eyes.

Moments later the bailiff was flying through the air with a flattened face, dozens of broken bones, a shredded uniform, and no hair. He crashed against the back wall of the courtroom so hard that one of his ears fell off.

Immediately, corrupt policemen and on-the-take city officials rushed into the courtroom and jumped on Loose Cannon, in an attempt to subdue the unruly witness. But nothing can subdue Loose Cannon, Private Eye, once he gets going. Even he can't stop himself.

Policemen began flying through windows, doors, and walls, spectators were thrown through each other, jurors were beaten to dust, evidence was torn up, and fires were set, both large and small. Loose Cannon was in a crimefighting frenzy. It was violent and a lot of it was pointless, but, as usual, it worked like a charm. Once it was all over and everyone had calmed down, and all the wreckage had been cleared away, and all the bodies had been identified, it was discovered that somehow the case had been solved.

As the judge was being led out of the courtroom in handcuffs, and the bailiff was being transported to the Ear Hospital, the Mayor arrived to shake Loose Cannon's angry hand.

"Loose Cannon, Private Eye, I don't know how you did it, but you've done it again," he said, admiringly. "And now that you've cleaned out the corrupt ninety percent of my administration, I, with my remaining henchmen, will be free to continue my fine fine work for the people of this city."

"You're going down too."

"What?"

"You're crooked too."

The Mayor began to sweat. "You're crazy."

"That's what you are, but what am I?"

The Mayor reeled, then shook a fist in Loose

Cannon's face. "Damn you and your acerbic wit!" He turned to his security team. "Apprehend this man!"

Ten minutes later the courthouse was a shambles, the people in the building across the street were unconscious, an airliner had been shot down, and the Mayor was being led away to pay the price (six months house arrest on his yacht) for his lifetime of dishonesty.

"Smooth move, Ex-Lax," said Loose Cannon.

I closed the book.

That was the way to act, I thought. That's what a private eye should be. Tough. Rude. Uncompromising. A man who's not afraid to defy society's conventions, disregard common courtesy, and make a farting sound at common sense, in the pursuit of justice.

Loose Cannon was the greatest hard-boiled detective of them all, in my opinion. He drank more liquor, beat up more people, and solved more crimes with less explanation than any detective in any series of books anywhere. He was a terror to criminals, an annoyance to the law, a delight to the whisky industry, and a man who always came out on top. True, his dialogue wasn't very clever, kind of childish really, strictly schoolyard stuff, but that just made him seem all the tougher. You have to be a pretty tough guy to get away with talking like a fourth grader. And he was tougher than anybody. He was my hero. He was my ideal.

I'd just discovered the Loose Cannon books,

though they'd been coming out regularly for quite awhile. There were dozens of them out there now, each one more exciting than the last. And I was inspired by them. He made it all seem so easy.

Loose Cannon wasn't one of those "thinking detectives" you run into in most detective books. He didn't waste time using his brain. He solved his cases now, before the facts even had time to get to his brain. When he got going on a case he didn't investigate anything. He just started swinging his fists and firing his gun and kept doing it until the case was solved. And it worked every time. And according to the flyleaf, all the stories in the Loose Cannon books were "based on, or inspired by, exaggerations of real or imagined events". So this wasn't something that was just all made up. There was some truth in there somewhere. It proved you could be a great detective without doing any thinking at all, if you set your mind to it. Like I said, I was inspired.

Inspiration was something I needed a lot of around this time, because my detective career was stalled again. No money, no clients, nothing. You've heard it all before, if you've read and enjoyed my previous memoirs, because that's the way my detective career has been going from day 6 (I took the first five days of my career off. "Sick relative", was the excuse I think I used. Or "Dead neighbor". One of those). Anyway, I hadn't had any cases at all this month, and my rent was almost due again. I needed to get something going here.

It's not like there weren't any crimes that needed to be solved. There were plenty of them around town to choose from. Corpses lying around everywhere. But nobody wanted me to investigate any of them. "How about this one?" I would say, pointing at an easy looking corpse that nobody had started on yet. "Anybody mind if I solve this one?" "No," they would say, "Leave it alone. That's Phil's." "Well how about that smelly one in the corner?" "Beat it, Burly," they would say. It seemed like that was the only thing anybody in Central City knew how to say anymore: "Beat it, Burly." I wish I had a million dollars for every time somebody has said that to me. I could retire.

My basic problem was, most people didn't consider me to be a real detective. Real detectives solve crimes, they felt. I didn't, they noticed. Most people just thought of me as some fat stupid guy who gets in the way all the time. (That's them talking, not me). When the newspapers mentioned me, which was rare, they usually put quotation marks around the word "detective", sometimes adding a pointing finger and a laughing face, or little drawings of stick figures holding their noses. That galled me, as the truth so often does.

That's why I was really studying the Loose Cannon books. Not just reading them for enjoyment and inspiration, but also taking notes and committing entire chapters to memory. I wanted to become a better detective. A detective people would respect. And write books about. And pay. And what better role model to have than the most successful detective ever? After reading several of the books it became clear to me where I had been making my mistake all these years. I was too brainy. That was the problem. I needed to adopt a less cerebral approach. Brawn, not brains, from now on. Action, not words. Fists, not friends.

I made a list of good simple hard-boiled things to say in various situations, practiced sneering in the mirror and giving myself the finger, then went out to try out my new technique.

I came back to my office with two black eyes, a red nose and a green mouth (somebody had crammed grass in there). One of my arms was in a sling, and a wisecrack had been shoved up my ass. Took me an hour to get it back out, which really made me mad because it didn't make any sense.

Okay, so I still had some work to do. There was something wrong with my technique. That was pretty obvious. But I would master it eventually. Rome wasn't built in a day, they tell me. Which I guess means we don't have to actually get anything done today, if we want to keep up with Rome. We've got an extra day to work with. We can take today off if we want. I guess that's what they mean when they say that. Though I wish they would just tell us straight out what they mean. I see no need for riddles. Like I always say, like I have printed on my coffee mug: "Life isn't a game. If it was, I would get a turn."

I pulled out my Loose Cannon notes again and went back to work practicing the tough-guy dialogue I had copied out of the books. I was getting better at it the more I practiced. I could blurt out: "That's what you are, but what am I?" with 80% accuracy, in two-tenths of a second, which I think is probably a world record time. At that speed all the words were so jammed together it just sounded like I had burped suddenly. I was trying to lower my world record time even farther when a prospective client came into my office.

"Mr. Burly?"

"That's who I am, but who are you?"

He looked at me blankly for a moment, then said: "Gesundheit."

I invited him to sit down and tell me his problem, but warned him that I was a busy, hard-boiled, man, so no bullshit, all right? Get to the point, make the check out to "Frank Burly", and get out. Tough, see? Uncompromising. That's what you get when you hire Frank Burly.

He started to explain what his problem was and why he wanted a detective, while I took notes and made whatever uncompromising comments and rude noises seemed appropriate, but after awhile my tough guy attitude and 4th Grade dialogue began to irritate him.

"I don't think I like your attitude," he finally said. "And I definitely don't like you giving me the finger."

I looked down at my Loose Cannon notes. "Tough toenails," I said.

He stood up. "You sir, are impertinent!"

"That better not mean what I think it means."

"It means I'm taking my business elsewhere." He stormed out of my office.

"Goodbye, Ex-Lax!" I called after him.

I frowned. That didn't go well. Fortunately, Rome wasn't built in two days either. It took over a month to build it. So I still had time. I was still ahead of schedule. I leaned back and put my feet up on my desk.

A month later my secretary poked her head into my office.

"A Professor Moriarty here to taunt you, sir."

I had never heard of him. But I'd talk to anybody at this point.

"Send him in."

CHAPTER TWO

A tall, well-dressed, urbane looking man came in, exuding bland smirking self confidence. I liked him already.

"What can I do for you, Mr. Moriarty?" I asked, as pleasantly as I could, as he made himself comfortable in my best chair, then used his cane to open the blinds a little, look out, then let them fall again. I had had a month to reflect on how I'd handled my last potential client, and had come to the conclusion that I had come on too strong too soon with that one. My no-nonsense manner, rude language, and threatening gestures had alienated him somehow. This time I would try to be nicer. There would still be plenty of time to be rude and uncompromising once I had actually been hired.

"Professor Moriarty," he said, correcting me, "I am a professor of Fourth Grade Mathematics at Central City Elementary School."

"Any relation to the Professor Moriarty in the Sherlock Holmes stories?"

"Only in spirit. Both the original Moriarty and myself have extraordinary mental powers, being endowed by nature with phenomenal mathematical faculties. We both are unknown to the police, walk the streets of the city unchallenged—aye, there's the genius and the wonder of the thing—and yet we are both criminal masterminds."

"You both use a lot of the same dialogue, too. I hope everything you've just said is in the public domain."

"It is."

"Good, because we don't need that kind of trouble. Say, would you mind turning off the sinister music?"

"If you insist." He reached into his coat pocket and switched off a small tape recorder he had in there. "My use of the name 'Professor Moriarty' is an homage, if you will."

"That's French for 'theft', isn't it?"

"Yes. You see, when I decided to become a criminal mastermind this morning the name Lawrence Sneed didn't have the right ring to it somehow. It didn't sound 'mastermindy' enough, if you see what I mean. So I borrowed the name of my illustrious predecessor."

I nodded. I understood changing your name to fit the business you're in. I had done the same thing myself, lots of times—changing my name to "Rock Bottom", to underline my reasonable price, then to "I. Possibly Solvecase", to give people the impression that I solved cases on occasion, and yours might be one of them, and "Topsy Turvey", to back up my advertising claim that I turned the criminal world upside down. None of them did me much good, though. Finally I settled on "Frank Burly", which didn't really get me much of anything either, but I was tired of changing it. Getting a new name painted on the door every other week was bankrupting me. And when people asked me who I was, I usually didn't know.

"I didn't want any trouble from the Conan Doyle Estate," Moriarty went on, "so I have styled myself 'Professor Moriarty 2', with a silent '2'. You can't hear it, but it's there."

I looked at the card he had given me. "I don't see a '2' on here."

"It is also invisible."

"Ah." I wrote in a small "2" at the end of his name so I would remember. "You say you became a criminal mastermind only this morning?"

"Yes."

"Why?"

A shadow passed over his face. His suave urbane countenance became grim. "I was passed over for promotion to the fifth grade level this morning, that's why. I have been left back to teach the fourth grade for yet another year, that's why. Incompetence! Professional jealousy! Fools! I'm surrounded by fools!"

I saw what probably had happened. "Maybe you weren't promoted because you're no good," I suggested.

"Nonsense."

"But..."

"I'm very good. Stupendous."

"Ah."

"So I have decided—as soon as a suitable replacement can be found—to leave education to the jealous little men who do that sort of thing, and move into a more rewarding field for a man of my extraordinary talents."

The guy was starting to make me tired. He sure liked himself. More than I did. What did he want, anyway? "Well that's all very interesting, probably," I said, "but why tell me? What did you come here for, anyway?"

"To inform you that I am about to perpetrate the Crime of the Century right under your very nose."

"I don't care."

"It will be the crowning achievement of my career."

"Yeah, well, do it outside."

He lit another cigarette. "What will it be? A bank robbery? No, too ordinary. The theft of a famous jewel, like the Dwight D. Eisenhower Diamond? Nothing so small as that. This will be a crime that staggers humanity. I tell you this because you are my enemy, and we..."

I had been starting to lose interest, like I always do when people aren't talking about me, but that caught my attention. That was about me. "I'm your enemy?"

"Yes."

"Well this is the first I've heard of it. Why me?"

13

He frowned. "To be perfectly honest, you have become my enemy by default. None of the other detectives would have anything to do with me—the fools."

"I don't want to have anything to do with you either. And yet, I am not a fool. Sometimes I appear to be a fool," I went on, chattily, "but that's because I have what doctors call 'Lazy Brain'. It's a medical condition. I also have 'Unattractive Face Disease' or 'UFD'. I'm taking pills for that. But they're not working."

He wasn't even listening to me. "I couldn't even get past the other detectives' secretaries," he mused, bitterly. "They said I wasn't important enough. They told me to leave my name and number. In the wastebasket. Fortunately, you don't have the layers of security other, more successful, detectives have. So it has been decided. You shall be my enemy. Ours will be a classic battle between brains and brawn."

"Which one am I?"

"Brawn."

I nodded. That was me, all right.

"But I don't want an enemy," I pointed out. I had spotted the flaw in his argument.

"There's nothing you can do about it," he assured me. "It's done. Just like there is nothing you can do to stop the Crime of the Century, which will take place next Tuesday. That's just six days from now."

"Tuesday is four days from now."

"What?"

"Four days, not six. For a mathematics professor you sure have trouble with numbers."

He counted on his fingers for a moment, frowned, then said: "You try to get that close." He flicked cigarette ash at my ashtray, missing it by several inches. "But no matter how many days away it is, a fool like you can do nothing to stop me." He looked at me with scorn. "You fool."

I thought about what Loose Cannon would do in a situation like this. I stood up. "I can beat your brains out," I said, cracking my knuckles. "That might stop you. You won't get very far without brains. At least not in any particular direction."

Professor Moriarty smiled blandly. He lit up a cigarette, with unconcern.

"I anticipated that. I wouldn't have come here alone and unarmed if I hadn't taken certain precautions first. If you harm me in any way, if you beat my brains out even this far," he held his fingers close together, "your friend will die."

"Huh?" My fists stopped pinwheeling, inches from his brain.

"He's being shadowed by my operatives right now," continued Professor Moriarty, lighting up several more cigarettes. He always looked more suave when he was lighting a cigarette, and he knew it, so he kind of overdid it. My smoke alarms had been going off ever since he came in, and my office was full of smoke rings. "I have left instructions that if I do not return by a certain time, your friend is to be killed."

"I don't have any friends."

Professor Moriarty looked startled. "None at all?"

"No."

He put out his cigarettes and started to rise. "Then, in that case..."

He picked up his hat and cane, and started for the door. I went with him to see him out and happened to glance out of the window. "Hey, criminal mastermind..." I said.

"Yes?"

"Your car is being towed away."

"Damn!" He looked down at the street. "So's yours."

I looked closer. "Shit."

"Damn," said Professor Moriarty.

"Shit," I said.

"Damn."

"Shit."

"Piss."

"Ass."

"Damn."

The typing in the next office stopped and there was a knocking on the wall.

"Stop all that swearing in there!" shouted someone.

Moriarty and I both lapsed into a sullen silence. There wasn't much left to say, except "shit", and we couldn't say that.

As Moriarty left he turned back to me and said: "Remember what I said about your friend."

"I'll remember," I said, confidently. I may not

be able to use my brain for much, but it is good for storage. I would remember about my friend, all right. I would put the memory of him back in the corner of my brain where I was remembering all those old magazines. Then I thought: hey, what friend? I don't have any friends. We've already established that.

But it looked like I did have an enemy.

CHAPTER THREE

So, as if I didn't have enough trouble of my own making (those forged checks come to mind. And that threatening letter I wrote to the Luftwaffe), now I had some kind of crazy enemy to deal with. Figures. The late Jimmy Hatlo was right about when things happen. They happen every time.

I knew from my reading that it wasn't unusual for private investigators to have to deal with personal enemies from time to time. Sherlock Holmes had his Moriarty. And Loose Cannon had an enemy too—Ned Nucleus, Crime Boss of the Ionosphere—an enemy who was just as over-the-top as he was. In the book I read, Ned Nucleus was trying to steal all of the world's Astroturf, and the only man who could stop him was Loose Cannon. Well, he stopped him, all right, but not until the last page. That's how close it was. Ned Nucleus was a worthy adversary for Loose Cannon. He was just as tough, and just as mean. You could always tell where they were fighting because of all the mushroom clouds and shrieking women.

The more I thought about it, the more having an enemy actually sounded like it might be kind of fun. Jumping out of hiding places at each other and crushing each others' skulls, pointing laser beams at each others' crotches to get each other to talk, killing each others' friends as fast as we made them, and so on. It wouldn't be dull, that's for sure. But I just didn't have the time for that sort of thing. Hey, I have to earn a living here.

Fortunately, I didn't see how Moriarty could actually make me do anything. He could say we were enemies all he wanted. So what? I'd just ignore him, the way everybody ignores me when I say I'm a detective. If he wanted to commit the "Crime of the Century", let him. He wasn't going to get me involved in it one way or the other. I just wasn't interested. And that was that.

The next day I received a phone call.

"Hello?" I said. There was no reply. I heard sinister music on the line. "Is that you, Moriarty?"

"Five days, Burly," he said. "Five days until the Crime of the Century."

"Three days," I said, correcting him.

"What?"

"Three days until the Crime of the Century. Invest in a pocket calculator or something. And I don't care when it is. I don't even know you. Quit calling here."

I hung up.

The following day he called again.

"Four days, Burly."

"Two," I said.

He was silent for a moment, then said: "In two days I will strike."

"Fine."

I hung up. Immediately, the phone rang again.

"Hey, are you going to try to stop me or not?" he asked.

"No."

"Why not?"

"I told you. We're not enemies. And nothing you can say or do is ever going to make us enemies."

"Oh no?"

"No."

I hung up the phone. That settled that. All you have to do is take a hard line with these people. Be firm. That's my secret, anyway.

Pleased that I had gotten Moriarty out of the way for good, I went downstairs for lunch. I almost didn't come back.

Everything at the diner seemed normal at first, except everybody was looking at me, but when my food arrived I didn't like the look of it.

"Your order, sir," said the waiter, as he put the plate with its festering contents down in front of me with a big pair of tongs. "Be careful, sir," he said, from behind his gas mask, "the plate is hot."

I took a bite, chewed it for a minute thoughtfully, then quickly spit it out.

"This is terrible! What is this?"

"It's the Fast-Acting Poison of the day, sir. With Sauce."

"I didn't order poison. I ordered the ham and eggs."

He gave me a perplexed look. "You didn't order it?"

"No."

The waiter went to the kitchen to investigate. He returned a few moments later, his gas mask stretched into a smile.

"It's all right, sir," he said. "Your order was changed."

"By who?"

"He didn't leave his name, but he was a tall urbane looking gentleman, wearing an 'I'm Frank Burly's Enemy' t-shirt."

So that was it. Moriarty.

"Yeah, well, I'm not paying for this."

His smile faded. "Oh yes you are."

After a lengthy heated discussion, in which the manager and several tough-looking cooks carrying cleavers joined in, I left the diner carrying the poison in a doggy bag. As long as I had to pay for it, I might as well take it with me. Maybe I could poison somebody back at the office with it.

As I crossed the street, a bullet tore the bag out of my hand. The next bullet took my left eyebrow off.

I looked across the street and raised my remaining eyebrow. A man I'd never seen before was sitting on the curb calmly firing a rifle at me. I walked over to him while he was reloading.

"Hey, what's the idea?" I asked.

"It's a joke," he said.

"A joke?" I pointed at my missing eyebrow. "You call this a joke? You're not funny, you know that?"

He shrugged. "I didn't think it was very funny, either. But your friend who paid me to do it said it was hilarious. Kind of an 'in-joke'. He said you'd get the humor of it."

"Well I don't!"

"Oh." He looked uncertain. "Should I keep reloading, or...?"

"No! You've done enough already."

"Because he paid me to shoot you until five o'clock."

"No, I said!"

I stalked angrily back across the street to see if my bag of poison was all right (it wasn't), and was nearly run over by a bus driven by a laughing driver. Another "joke" of Moriarty's, presumably. Well I didn't get that one either.

When I got home that night, my house was on fire. And all the retardant in my fire extinguishers had been replaced with gasoline and spiders. Moriarty, again.

I knew what he was trying to do, of course. He was trying to make me mad enough to fight back. But I wasn't going to do it. You can't manipulate Frank Burly that easily. Now that I knew what he was up to, I was determined that he wasn't going to make me mad. No matter what he did from now on, I wasn't going to let it bother me. I would just laugh it off.

The next day I laughed while people shot at me, guffawed as buildings fell on me, and blew milk and blood out of my nose with laughter every time someone hit me in the back of the head. It was tough for me to laugh off some of these attacks because I was so badly injured the paramedics said if I laughed one more time I might die, but I managed it anyway. Moriarty wasn't making me mad today. Oh, no. I'm too smart.

But finally it got to be too much, even for a man who is as patient and as hard to manipulate as I am. When I found myself flat on my back in the middle of the street with a paid assassin trying to drill a hole in my head with a hand drill, and another paid assassin biting my foot as hard as he could, while two dynamite trucks took turns rolling over me, I decided I'd had enough. I couldn't laugh this sort of thing off any longer. I was laughed out. I decided to just have it out with Moriarty right now, once and for all. If he wanted an enemy, he had one. Let's get this over with, so we can all get back to work. That's the way I felt.

Moriarty had said that he worked at Central City Elementary School, which was on the other side of town. So when the next bus tried to run over me, I got on it.

Central City Elementary is a big school, so it took me awhile to find the classroom Moriarty was in. A lot of the kids were kicking me as I wandered through the halls. I wondered why. A new fad, maybe. I hoped it wouldn't last long. Finally I turned around and found there was a "Kick Me" sign on my back. I tore it off, angrily, then, after a moment's reflection, put it back on, after changing it to read: "Kick Me And Hire Me".

Then I heard Moriarty's smugly complacent voice coming through the door of one of the classrooms. I slowly opened the door, just a crack, then inserted part of my face into this crack. I couldn't see much, because my eyes were still outside, just my nose was in there—I can't see through my nose like Loose Cannon can—so I pushed more of my face into the room. Now I could see everything in the room really well, including all the kids' faces looking at me.

Moriarty was writing something on the blackboard and had his back to me, so I edged into the room, making as little noise as possible, found a seat, removed the kid who was sitting there, sat down, and waited, arms folded. Now I had him.

"So, as you can see, children," Professor Moriarty was saying, as he finished writing out an equation, "when you add up the numbers in this equation, the answer is 'about seven'". All the kids wrote this approximation down. So did I. Seven, eh?

Moriarty turned away from the blackboard and saw me sitting in the third row.

"I see we have a new student," he said.

I made a noncommittal sound that was neither a "yes" nor a "no", but sounded a lot like "yes".

"Perhaps our new student would like to tell the class how much 6 plus 5 is."

"A million," I said.

Everybody laughed. I did, too. Hey, mathematics is fun! It's fun getting the right answer.

But after we had all been laughing for awhile, I realized that everyone was laughing at me, not with me. We weren't laughing with delight at my correct answer. We were laughing with scorn at how wrong my answer had been. That made me mad. Somebody should have told me what we were laughing about.

Moriarty asked me the question again, giving me another chance to get it right, but this time my answer was even further from the mark, judging by the class' reaction.

"Nebraska," I said.

The kids laughed at me even more this time. The bell rang, indicating the class was over, but none of the kids wanted to leave. They were having too good of a time. They wanted to hear me answer more questions. I wasn't having a good time, though. I was starting to get steamed. So I retaliated. I started laughing at them. I laughed at how short they were, and how awkward they were, especially you girls over there, and how poor their families must be to dress them like that, and they started crying, because it was all true.

The principal really told me off for the way I'd acted in class. I said they had laughed at me first, and I was the one hurt most by the laughter, but he insisted on singling me out for punishment. I didn't think that that was fair then, and I don't think it's fair now.

After he'd made me sit in his office staring at the corner for awhile, I pointed out that I wasn't actually a student at the school, so I shouldn't be subject to its horseshit rules and regulations, but he just made me sit in a worse corner for saying horseshit.

"I guess this must be Horseshit Corner," I said.
"Silence!"
"But..."
"There is no talking in Horseshit Corner!"

By the time I finally managed to get out of there the school day was over. Everyone had gone home, including Moriarty. So I went home too.

The next morning when I showed up for class—this time I wasn't going to sit in the third row. This time I was going to sit on Moriarty—I found out I wasn't allowed in the school anymore. I had been expelled. I protested, but it didn't get me anywhere. Finally, a nine year old hall monitor showed up and told me to hit the road.

Since I couldn't get in to see Moriarty where he worked, and I didn't know where he lived (he wasn't in that post office box listed on his business card. Nobody was. Just some mail in there), I decided to go back to my office and wait for him to make the next move. That cheered me up. I like waiting for people to make the next move. I'm good at it.

I'd just gotten myself some coffee and a donut

and had put my feet up on my desk as far as they would go, which is how I wait for people to make the next move, when a man rushed into my office wearing a mask and looking at his watch.

Ah, good, I thought. A client. And a wealthy one, judging by the dollar sign painted on his empty sack. I invited him to sit down, take off his mask, and tell me his problem. Maybe he was having trouble getting the mask off and that's why he was here. I could help him with that, for a price. Whatever his problem was, he had come to the right place.

The man didn't say anything. He just kept looking at his watch. Which eventually caused me to start looking at mine. Is it time for something? I didn't want to miss out on anything. I asked him if he wanted some coffee. He shook his head slightly, still intent on looking at his watch. Then he suddenly leaned across my desk— with me leaning towards him to see what was up— and knocked me over with a blackjack. Then he stole the contents of my office safe ($62!), ate my donut (jelly-filled!), and rushed out again. I had been robbed! In my own office! And knocked over! Out of my own swivel chair! It was humiliating. I was glad Loose Cannon wasn't here to see this. Or his sidekick Crazy Boy, either.

CHAPTER FOUR

I went outside, rubbing my head, to see which way the robber had gone. But I couldn't see him anywhere. In fact, I couldn't see anything. It had suddenly gotten completely dark, right in the middle of the day. It was a total eclipse!

I heard: "hands up" and "this is a robbery" and "hands up for the robbery" from hundreds of gruff voices all up and down the street. A few moments later all the streetlights popped on, and I saw that every store, every bank, every business of any kind in town, had a blinking robber standing in front of it holding a gun and a money sack.

Everything was being robbed! Or at least that's what was supposed to be happening. Evidently whoever had planned this heist, and I could guess who it was, had timed the eclipse perfectly, but had forgotten about streetlights.

Well, Professor Moriarty had told me that he was going to commit the Crime of the Century. And it looked like this was it. He was apparently attempting to steal the whole city at once, under cover of darkness. He had rented men—some with the price tags still hanging from them, some still in their original cellophane wrapping—poised and ready to go in front of every building in town, waiting for the darkness that had come and, just as quickly, gone.

It was a daring plan, but those streetlights coming on had ruined everything. As all criminals know, it's hard enough stealing something when no one can see you. It's murder in broad daylight, when everyone is watching (and criticizing) every move you make. So most criminals prefer darkness when they can get it. Of course, everything is locked up when it's dark, so you can't steal as much then. It's kind of a trade-off. That's why an eclipse is so perfect for a robber. Dark, but doors open. This robbery looked like the work of a learned man, one who could figure out the timing on an eclipse, but also the work of a beginner, one who could overlook a small, but important, detail, like streetlights. This looked like the work of Professor Moriarty to me.

I was also pretty sure that this was the work of Professor Moriarty because there he was, right over there, kicking his rented men's backsides trying to get them going. But they wouldn't, or couldn't, move. They were all just standing there, staring up at the streetlights with their mouths hanging open.

Alarms were beginning to sound all over town, and police cars were rushing in every direction, sirens wailing, but still the robbers wouldn't move. All of them ended up being caught in the act, most of them with their mouths still open. The only one who didn't get caught was the guy who had robbed me. His watch must have been fast. That's why he got away.

"Hey, you! Moriarty!" I yelled. "Give me back my 62 bucks!"

"It's the Crime of the Century!" he said, defiantly waving the $62 at me.

"I concede that, but give it back. I need it."

"Won't!"

Well, I knew what Loose Cannon would do in a situation like this. It happened in all of his books, usually on about page 2. This was the point where he would stop bandying words with the criminal and start taking action. Violent mindless action. So that's what I did. I started running at Moriarty, roaring and swinging my fists around in huge circles.

He took one look at me, and another at all the police cars heading his way, then took off running, still triumphantly waving my $62.

It was a grand chase. The Chase of the Century. We went from one end of Central City to the other, with me huffing and puffing all the way, and he gliding along with a suave self-satisfied smile on his face. It's difficult to appear bland and evil while you're running as fast as you can, but Professor Moriarty managed it. He had style, I'll give that to him.

But style is no match for determination when

it comes to the chase. Every time he thought he was well away and could sit down at a sidewalk café with a glass of wine and start counting my money, I would come huffing around the corner, and the chase would be on again.

Sometimes he tried to hide from me, but, true to form, as a beginning master criminal, with still a lot to learn yet, he never managed to hide himself completely from a trained eye like mine. I'd always see at least part of his rear end sticking out.

Finally the chase took us to the Central City Convention Center, where, according to the marquee out front, they were holding the "4th Annual Scientist's Convention—The 'Checking Your Work Expo'".

Professor Moriarty raced in without paying, which caused consternation in the ticket booth, a consternation that doubled when I breezed through.

When I got inside and had checked my hat and coat, and put on my visitor's badge, and leafed through the program of today's events, and had gotten a drink and chatted briefly with another guest, explaining to him that I felt that checking your work was a waste of time because the guy who's checking the work is just as stupid as the guy who originally did the work, that was the thing that everybody forgot, I found that I had lost Moriarty completely. Still, he had to be in here someplace, so I started wandering around, looking the place over with a magnifying glass, and asking everybody I bumped into if they'd seen anybody with $62 around here.

Like everything that has anything to do with science or learning, the Convention was incredibly boring. The entertainment, if you can call it that, was a blackboard with a hilariously wrong equation on it: $E=MC^{2.6}$. When the fun started to flag you could always look at the blackboard and have a good laugh. Everyone who wasn't laughing at the joke, or standing in line waiting to laugh at the joke, was standing around quietly in small boring groups, talking in a monotone about things that didn't mean anything at all, and weren't interesting to anybody.

"Did you know," said one scientist to another, "that the words I'm saying to you now will never be heard on Mars?"

"Is that a fact?"

"Yes. It's a fun fact."

"It is rather fun."

The head scientist at the convention, a rather pleasant young man named Doctor Smiley, intercepted me and asked if there was anything he could do to help me. Like, did I need any help picking up the experiments and Convention guests I had knocked over? And did I want to pay for those things I had been putting in my pocket? I asked him if he'd seen a master criminal around here. He was about so high, and he would be carrying $68 that wasn't his. ($62 didn't sound impressive enough to me anymore. It was too true. So I bumped it up to $68.) Doctor Smiley said he hadn't seen anyone like that. He didn't think master criminals were even allowed on the premises. But if he did run into him he would let me know. In the meantime, did I want to borrow his deodorant? The reason he asked was...

After I had finished with Doctor Smiley (I really smell nice now), and just as I was knocking over a large display of "Inventions That Will Never Be Knocked Over", I spotted Professor Moriarty. He was unsuccessfully hiding behind a large plexiglass beaker. The only part of him that was visible to the naked eye was his huge contorted face. But that was enough.

I took off after him, pinwheeling my fists.

"Moriarty!" I roared.

He quickly got behind a large circular conference table and began moving around it, this way and that, taunting me, as I tried to figure out a way to get to him.

"What's the matter? Can't you get around the table?" he sneered.

"I guess not. Or when I do, then you're not there anymore."

"Ha!"

Frustrated with my inability to get my hands on Moriarty when he was so close, I started emptying test tubes into the punch bowl and throwing them at him, while the scientists watched, sipping their punch.

After I had finally nailed him good with one of the test tubes, he got mad and started hurling stuff back at me. I guess he had a better arm than I did because he hit me four or five times for every time I hit him. And all of his throws were coming in pretty fast. I think it was the cash register that finally finished me off.

When I regained consciousness a little while later, Moriarty was long gone. The scientists who helped me to my feet, I noticed, were starting to act a little more interesting now than they had been before. They were twitching a lot, and their noses were vibrating like dentists' drills. Their grins were growing more lopsided every second. And their eyes had the light of madness in them.

"Did anybody see where that guy went?" I asked, brushing off my clothes into the punch. "That guy with the major league fastball?"

"No," replied a scientist, sipping more punch.

"Damn," I said, petulantly kicking a jar of chemicals into the punch, then angrily stirring it around.

"Do you feel funny?" asked one of the scientists, sipping his punch.

"I feel hilarious," said the other, sipping his punch.

"I'm feeling funnier by the minute," said another, looking at his watch.

One by one, the scientists began throwing back their heads and laughing.

I didn't know what was so funny, but whatever it was, it was obvious that this was the highlight of their whole day, so far. It was The Laugh of the Convention.

I was glad somebody was having a good time.

CHAPTER FIVE

"Stick 'em up!" said Loose Cannon, Private Eye.

"But I've got the gun," protested the criminal. "If anybody's going to be putting their hands up, it should be you."

"You won't stick 'em up?"

"I don't think I should."

"You asked for it, Ex-Lax."

Loose Cannon leaped onto the criminal, ignoring the flying bullets and thrown gun, and hit the criminal's nose so hard it bent up and hit the criminal in the eye. Then he bashed the criminal's nose down into his mouth, following this with a terrific uppercut so the criminal bit his own nose off. Then he began beating the criminal to pieces with the criminal's own fists, saying: "Why are you hitting yourself? Why are you hitting yourself?" Then: "Why are you eating yourself? Why are you eating yourself?" Followed by: "Why are you hanging yourself? Why are you hanging yourself?"

And the criminal didn't say anything. He

wouldn't be saying anything for a long time. For he was dead. As dead as a corpse.

I closed the book. That was the way to deal with criminals. That was the way to deal with everybody. Kill 'em all, and let God read them their rights.

The more I read the Loose Cannon books the more impressed I was by them. They were full of great crimefighting tips, loaded with juvenile dialogue, and the stories were exciting too. The only complaint I had about the books were the deceptive titles. "Rat In The Refrigerator" for example, is a top notch thriller, Loose Cannon at his surly angry best, but it has nothing to do with what you see on the garish cover until the final sentence in the book, which is: "At least we could be thankful for one thing; at least there wasn't a RAT IN THE REFRIGERATOR!" They shouldn't be allowed to trick you like that with their teaser covers. Don't get me wrong. It was a good book. It just didn't have enough rats in it.

I put away the book and compared my latest adventure, tentatively titled: "Untitled Adventure Number Forty", to Loose Cannon's latest adventure. Mine was less satisfying. No doubt about that. I hadn't killed anybody. Or arrested anybody. Everybody in my adventure had gotten away. I hadn't solved any mysteries. I never do. And the Queen of England hadn't knighted me and offered to move in to my apartment with me, like she had with Loose Cannon. There was a rat in my refrigerator, but that was the only similarity between the two stories.

I tried to be philosophical about it. Okay, so Professor Moriarty had ended up getting away from me. Fine. That's what I wanted him to do. Get away from me. The farther he got away from me the better. Plus, though I hadn't personally foiled it, his plan had been a failure. His eclipse idea had been good, but he had forgotten one little detail—streetlights. I didn't laugh at him for that. I'd forgotten about streetlights too. When did this city get streetlights? Neat.

With Moriarty out of my hair now, hopefully at least until the next eclipse, I got back to work. I started walking the streets with my "Kick Me And Hire Me" sign on my back, hoping to drum up some business. But it didn't get me anything. A few people kicked me, but that was as close as I got to a job. I think people should read the whole sign on someone's back, not just part of the sign.

It was during these walks that I started noticing some odd creatures wandering around town. They were just shadows disappearing quickly into alleyways at first. Then I saw them walking along in crowds, trying to blend in. Then they grew bolder, riding in taxis, and leaning against lamp posts, making eerie whistling sounds at girls. They were very odd-looking creatures. I'm not sure what you would call them. Not monsters, certainly. They were too small for that. But they weren't exactly natural looking either. I'd certainly never seen anything like them.

One was sort of a double guinea pig, with ears on both ends. There was a rat with wheels, a rocket-frog, a gerbil who walked upright and was capable of ordering from a menu, and a rabbit that hopped both ways. Central City was being flooded with all kinds of bizarrely mutated lab animals. Fortunately, though they were all pretty crazy looking, none of them appeared to be particularly dangerous.

Other people noticed the odd creatures too, but they pretended they didn't. You know how it is. Slightly odd things, like somebody's nose running, people notice. When somebody's nose starts smiling, people go out of their way not to notice it. Just sell them their newspaper, or whatever, and move on to the next customer. That's the way most people handle it. Makes sense, too. If you don't notice something, it can't harm you.

I tried to ignore what was going on, too. I always try to do that if I can. It works. Try it. You'd be surprised how easy it is to ignore what's going on in this world of ours if you'll only try. And if I was confronted directly by one of the creatures I usually just said: "Nice doggy", which always seemed to satisfy it, whatever it looked like. Sometimes it wagged a tail I didn't know about.

But then one day one of the creatures did something I couldn't ignore. The little bastard ran off with my keys.

I took off after it, shouting at it to come back.

I needed those keys. My whole life was locked now. I couldn't get into any of it without my keys. I'd be stuck out here.

As I ran, I noticed the people on the street were not only ignoring the creature I was chasing, they were ignoring me too. I was a little offended by that. I look normal. You can notice me.

I followed the creature to the city's Convention Center, where I had lost Professor Moriarty during our grand chase, if you'll remember. It looked different to me now somehow. And after a few moments I realized what it was. Those turrets. That moat.

The scientists had been totally altering the appearance of the place, busily adding battlements, planting jungle undergrowth where the parking lot had been, and somehow turning the air around the place a little darker and more forbidding than the air anywhere else. The marquee outside said: "4th Annual Scientist's Convention. Day 6. Today – Stay Out."

I went to the main entrance. It had a sign on it that said: "Closed. No Admittance. Entry Forbidden." I studied this sign for a moment, then decided it probably didn't mean me. My name wasn't mentioned. I slicked back my hair and started to stroll in. The door was locked. I rattled it. It was more locked now. I rattled it one more time. Now it was locked forever.

I went around to the side of the building. Crates of radiation, cosmic rays, and lightning were being brought in by a side entrance. I jumped on a dolly and started being hauled in, but somebody saw me and told me to get off of there. I said I was an important box that was being delivered. But they said they hadn't just become deliverymen yesterday. They'd been deliverymen for as long as they could remember. And I wasn't a box. Boxes don't tell people they're boxes, and they don't say "This is the life" as they are being wheeled along. Instead of trying to argue with them, I just tried to look more like a box. But they weren't buying it. I had to get off.

I went back to the main entrance. Still locked. Locked more now. I looked up at the scientists on the ramparts. They all had a kind of twisted twitchy out-of-focus look on their faces, and didn't look like they would welcome visitors. Nonetheless, I hailed them and told them I had come for a visit.

"There's nobody home," one of them said.

"You're here."

"Go away."

"No."

The scientists conferred and then asked me what I wanted. I said I wanted to come inside. They said they weren't expecting visitors, and the place was a mess, but I said I was coming in anyway. Important Convention business. Besides, I was an important box that was being delivered. And my company—The Important Corporation—had just taken over their branch of science and I had been sent here by the main office to be their new boss. I would be stern, but fair, I promised them. But I would have to get in first. That clinched it. I was too important in too many different ways. They exchanged deranged looks, shrugged, then pressed a button that unlocked the door.

I went inside and found that the place was, indeed, a mess. They sure weren't expecting visitors. Sheesh. There were half-finished experiments piled high on every table, vials of weird serums and half-drunk cups of coffee that were being bombarded by cosmic rays and leaking all over the floor, and empty pizza boxes everywhere you tried to sit down. Plus, there were even more of the odd creatures wandering around here than there were in town. And these seemed even crazier than the first bunch I had seen. Ratacopters, pogo-mice, lab rabbits that were all ears, and an eye-chart with eyes. Everything seemed to be here except my keys.

I quickly stopped worrying about the keys, though. This was more interesting. This wasn't the usual boring kind of science and learning that I was used to—the kind that has been boring mankind to death for centuries. This was something altogether more interesting and sinister. There might be a real story here, I thought. A story I could sell to the newspapers. Maybe I could even use this as a springboard towards a new career in journalism. Those newspaper reporters make millions, they tell me.

I started taking notes, and getting candid shots of some of the weirder creatures, as well as some nice snapshots of myself next to some natural laws being broken, all the while muttering "What a story!" to myself, and humming the "What A Story Song". That's when some of the scientists came over to see what I was doing.

"May I help you?" asked one of the scientists, his bland, boring, face twitching like...I dunno....like some kind of living thing.

"No," I said, snapping a flashbulb in his face, "I can do it."

"What are you making notes about?" asked another scientist, whose eyes were going in circles.

"Nothing," I said, hastily putting away my notebook, and my spy camera, and my really big notebook with the spy camera on every page. "Nothing at all."

"Good," said the scientist, relieved.

We all relaxed. I searched for something to say.

"Looks like you're creating a chamber of horrors here," I said, conversationally.

"That's right," one scientist said proudly.

"Brad here deserves most of the credit," said another, pointing at one of the scientists, who had a jutting jaw and windblown hair.

"I couldn't have done it without you guys," said Brad, modestly.

"You're too modest, Brad."

"I couldn't be modest without you."

"Okay, that's enough, Brad."

"Well," I said, casually, edging towards the exit,

"now that I know too much, maybe I'd better leave."

A couple of scientists quickly stepped in front of me.

"What's this about knowing too much?" asked one, sharply.

"Too much about what?" asked another. "Not about us, I hope."

Doctor Smiley joined the group. His eyes lit up and blared like car horns when he saw me.

"Ah, it's you!" he said. "Did you ever find your enemy?"

"Yeah, but now I've got a bunch more enemies." I indicated the other scientists. "These guys won't let me leave."

"They won't?" His smile went down a notch.

He turned and had a long animated discussion with the scientists who were blocking my path, all of them sipping punch as they talked. During this discussion, a number of dark looks were directed my way. Every time they looked at me, I waved. They waved back, but very reluctantly. Finally Doctor Smiley turned back to me.

"It looks like we're going to have to imprison you, Mr. Burly."

I was disappointed to hear this. He saw the look of disappointment on my face.

"It's necessary, I'm afraid," he said, apologetically. "We really don't have any other choice."

"I could give you some other choices."

"Oh, good," he said, relieved. "Let's hear them."

All the scientists leaned forward.

"Oh... uh..." I hadn't expected this. "Well... you could elect me your leader. Then I could lead us all to freedom."

There was a brief discussion about this. A few of the scientists seemed to be willing to give it a try, but the majority were against it. Doctor Smiley turned back to me, regretfully.

"No, we don't like that idea so much." He sipped his punch. "And the punch says no."

"Do you have any other ideas?" asked one of the scientists, hopefully.

"No."

"Then you'll have to come along with us."

I started to resist, but several scientists quickly pulled out crazy looking experimental guns made out of mice and pointed them at me. I stopped resisting. Those mice were set to "Kill".

"What a story!" I said, as I was marched away to a makeshift dungeon in the bowels of the Convention Center.

"Silence!" said one of the scientists.

"Silence about the story," said another.

CHAPTER SIX

The "dungeon" they stuck me in was actually just a converted Day Care Center. It didn't look too tough to escape from, for an old hand like me, but when the scientists came in to check on me a few hours later, I was down on my hands and knees fooling around with some toys.

"Mr. Burly..."

"Just a minute. Let me finish this game."

They waited patiently for me to finish the game, then stopped me when I was about to start another one.

"We came to check on you and see how you're doing down here," said Doctor Smiley.

"Fine."

I went back to my game, but they stopped me again.

"What?" I asked, testily.

They looked embarrassed. "Well, frankly, now that we have you, we're not sure what to do with you."

I suddenly became alarmed. "Don't experiment on me!"

"Hey, that's an idea," said one of them. "Let's experiment on him!"

The other scientists were immediately sold on this idea.

"That would be great!" said one. "We've only had boring lab animals to experiment on up till now."

"A human! Oh boy, oh boy!" said another, rubbing his hands.

"Hey, wait a minute, guys," I said, holding up a hand. "I said 'don't' experiment on me. Not 'do'. 'Don't'. If you're not going to do exactly what I say, don't do what I say at all." But they were already dragging me out of the dungeon to get started on the experiments. Oh boy, me and my big experimental mouth.

They strapped me down on a long table and made me sign all the usual release forms—forms which released them from any responsibility in case something, like, went wrong, and somebody, for example, died. They didn't want to have to spend the rest of their lives paying for this if something went wrong. Then we were ready to go.

"Okay, let's get started," said Doctor Smiley.

The scientists all rubbed their hands and rolled up their sleeves, looked at me, rubbed their hands again, then seemed to draw a blank. They didn't know what to do next.

"Don't start with the scalpels!" I yelled, wildly.

"Hey!" said one of the scientists. "Let's start with the scalpels!"

"Good idea, Brad!"

I decided to keep my mouth shut after that. Stop giving them ideas. Brad would just take all the credit anyway.

They got their scalpels out, then there was a long delay while they tried to think of some experiments to do with them. They looked at me hopefully, but I wouldn't say anything. After another long pause they looked at me again. I shook my head.

Finally, Doctor Smiley suggested that they proceed with the experimentation as if I was something they were used to experimenting on. Like litmus paper.

That broke the logjam. That got them going. I could see why Doctor Smiley was their leader.

First they put me into a big test tube (the second biggest test tube I had ever seen) and started mixing me with various chemicals to see what would happen. They turned me different colors, vaporized part of me, then condensed me back into a solid, and dunked me in various acids to see what effect that would have on a detective. They even rearranged my limbs until they were all pointing towards magnetic north. They were having a blast. And, though some of the experiments hurt quite a bit, and I didn't at all like the way they had experimentally combed my hair, I was getting interested too.

"Try putting my teeth where my nuts are," I suggested. "See what that does."

"Quiet," said one of the scientists, severely. "We're the scientists, you're just the willing test subject." He held up the paper I had signed. "We'll decide which experiments to do."

"Hey! Let's put his teeth where his nuts are!"

"You've done it again, Brad," they said, admiringly.

"I nominate Brad for President of the Scientist's Council."

"Be quiet, Brad."

They went back to work on me. I forget what most of the other experiments were, because the last one involved taking my brain out, banging it on the table, flipping it over, and putting it back in, blindfolded. That one really wasn't much of an experiment. More of a parlor game.

Finally they ran out of ideas again. There are only so many things you can do with litmus paper, even a big piece like me. They started looking at me again for their next idea. I was getting tired of this.

"Hey, what kind of mad scientists are you?" I asked, exasperated. "Don't you guys have any imagination?"

They looked at each other.

"We've heard of it," one finally said.

"We can spell it," added another.

The rest nodded. They could spell it all right.

"Well, haven't you ever watched any science fiction movies?" I asked.

"Science FICTION movies!" said one.

"You mean movies that combine the thrilling rigidity of the scientific method with the unbridled creativity of fiction?" asked another scientist, clearly dazzled by the idea.

"Well, I'm not sure what they combine with what, but they call it science fiction."

The scientists got together and talked excitedly about this new (to them) concept, then started putting on their hats and coats.

"You'll have to excuse us for a little while," said Doctor Smiley.

"Take your time," I said. I wasn't going anywhere.

"There's coffee in the Half Rabbit/Half Coffee Pot."

"Thanks."

There was a long delay while the scientists went to the video store, finally returning late in the afternoon with armloads of rented movies, bags of popcorn, and a couple of girls.

Then they sat down and watched them all, from the earliest sci-fi silent films to the latest 3D blockbusters, getting more excited all the time, and saying things like: "Look at the size of that ant, will ya!" and "Now that's a good use for lightning!" and "Good thinking, Boris. Those villagers won't be back."

These movies opened up a whole new world to them. They showed what a mad scientist can really do if he puts his deranged mind to it. Inspired, they began building their own version of Frankenstein—to see if they could do it. The finished monster had some things wrong with it—it kept falling over backwards and catching fire, and its language was shocking—but it was a start. They immediately went to work on another, better, one. This one would have improved coordination, a built-in sprinkler system, and the mouth of a clergyman (if they could find one).

Soon they had their own versions of Dracula, Frankenstein, The Mummy, and Wolfman. They created giant insects, fire-breathing prehistoric monsters, various crawling human body parts with bad attitudes and big plans, all sorts of B-movie-type monsters. Everything they made was pretty similar to the monsters they'd seen in the movies. Similar enough that I was confident that somebody was going to sue their asses off before this was all over.

This was something that had apparently occurred to the scientists, too. And they were worried about it. After a number of anxious discussions, they finally decided to just do what Hollywood always does. They changed the monsters slightly, and gave them slightly different names like Frankenberg and Grabzilla. Then they gave them props to make them look a little different. And it worked. A small cap was all it took for Wolfman to become an entirely new character: "The Chauffeur of Wolfman". And when they put a sailor's hat on Frankenstein it instantly transformed him into "Captain Frankenstein". It was an easy fix, and its legality was firmly in a gray area, so that's the way they decided to go. From then on, they always made sure to change the idea enough so they were confident they wouldn't get sued, but not enough so that they wouldn't be able to think of it in the first place.

None of this experimentation was done with any concrete objective in mind. The scientists didn't plan to actually use the monsters for anything. It was the creating of the creatures that interested them. Once they were done making them, and had taken them for a trial spin or two, they ignored them, or stacked them in a spare room, or just allowed them to wander off somewhere, while they went back to work on another one. Pretty soon there were monsters of all different types and of varying quality everyplace you looked. There was a stack of defective Wolfmen in the corner, complaining about the dog food they were being given, and there were factory second Frankensteins walking in place up against a wall, with others dead in the kitchen.

It's fortunate that the scientists didn't want to use the monsters for anything in particular, because they were basically useless. The replicas were too perfect, that was the problem. Being Hollywood movie monsters, they mostly just stood around wanting to know what their motivation was, and bitching about the catering, and trying to call their agents to see what their next gig was after this. And it was no good telling them they didn't have an agent. Of course they had an agent. He just hadn't gotten back to them yet.

While I was waiting for the scientists to get back to me, I passed the time by chatting with a few of the monsters, arguing with them sometimes, poking them in the chest as I made my points. "And I'll tell you another reason why eating all the Republicans wouldn't work," I would say. When they asked me what kind of monster I was, I told them I was a "Half man/half dinosaur". They looked me over and asked what the dinosaur part was. I told them I was a dinosaur on the inside. They treated me with more respect after that. I was half dinosaur, they explained to any new monster who showed up. The dinosaur part was on the inside.

Finally I got tired of waiting around. I'd been strapped to the table for days. "Hey," I hollered, "Are you guys done with me?"

I should have kept my mouth shut, of course. Everybody should always keep their mouths shut. But for some reason mine keeps popping open, usually at the wrong time. I had hoped that now that they had more exciting things to experiment on they would let me go. But calling attention to myself just got them interested in me again. They came back and resumed experimenting on me, this time using their new found knowledge and expertise in the drive-in movie monster field.

Over the next few days they turned me into "The Detective From The Black Lagoon", "The Fat Guy From Haunted Hill", "Detecula", and their version of Lassie, which they called "Blassie". I tried to explain to them that Lassie wasn't actually a monster. All those Lassie pictures they had seen weren't considered monster movies. They were more "family fare". Somebody had obviously made a mistake at the video store. But the scientists just thought I was trying to tell them about some scientist who was trapped in a mine. That wasn't what I was trying to say at all. I barked louder, but they just kept looking in the mine again.

Then they made their big mistake. They turned me into "The Amazing Colossal Fifty Foot Detective". As soon as my body reached the fifty foot mark, I broke free of my bonds, hurled the surprised and disappointed scientists aside, and crashed out of the Convention Center.

"All right," I heard one of the scientists say as I stomped away, kicking aside security people and picking guard dogs off my chest, "whose idea was it to make him fifty feet tall?"

Everyone looked at Brad.

CHAPTER SEVEN

I bet you've been waiting for one of my books to have a happy ending. Well, so have I. And it looked like this was it. Not only was my life back to normal, it was nine times better than normal. Because I was nine times bigger than I was before. Fifty feet tall and all is well.

When I came back into town, the ground was shaking and plaster was falling from ceilings with every colossal step I took. It was kind of fun. Kiss your plaster goodbye, everybody, because the big guy is back in town.

People screamed when they first saw me, but after they had calmed down a little bit, and somebody had given them some water, they realized that it was just me. They'd seen me before. I wasn't anything to scream about, no matter how big I was. So, after another glass of water, and after assuring everybody they were all right now, they went back to ignoring me like they had always done before.

That frosted me a little, and I thought of maybe

stepping on a couple of their houses for them, kind of accidental-like. Ignore me, will you? See how you like living in a flat house. See how you like taking your showers lying down. And carrying your pets around in your wallet. And inviting your guests to "crawl on in". See how you like that. Well, they wouldn't like it, of course. And, though they would definitely show me a lot more respect, they'd probably call the cops on me too. Then I might end up having to step on some cops. So I decided I'd better not cause any trouble. I had a happy ending going here. I didn't want to screw it up.

But when I got home I discovered my new life wasn't quite as perfect as I thought it was. This wasn't a happy ending yet. I still had some problems I had to deal with. I couldn't get through my front door, for one thing. Damn thing was too small. Had to go in the back door. And once I got inside, I found that the whole place was too small for me. I could only get two fingers into the kitchen, for example, and then I couldn't get the tiny can opener to work on any of my tiny cans. So, no dinner tonight. And I'm not going to even talk about the bathroom. Let's put it this way: I'm never going in that bathroom again. Too much shit in it.

All my furniture was too small for me now, too. And, hey, I just wrecked my bed. Problems? I had a house full of them.

Even the television was too small for me. My giant eyes couldn't tell what was going on on most of the shows. I finally had to change it to the Close-Up Channel ("All Close-Ups All The Time"). That helped a little, but the picture still seemed awfully small to me. And those dramas they have on the Close-Up Channel aren't very good. ("What's that you are doing with your hands, Mr. Wilkerson?" "Pan down and see, Mildred.")

I ended up having to order new custom-made everything: oversized furniture, stadium-sized TV, special three foot long toothbrushes, you name it. And that custom made stuff doesn't come cheap, you know. A giant toothpick costs a lot more than a regular toothpick. Take it from me. I learned that the hard way. Now I knew how the Government felt when it bought things. Like that toilet seat they paid $3000 for. Remember that? I'm guessing it was really big—big enough for the whole Government to sit on at once—which is why it cost so much. Probably saved the taxpayers money in the long run, but at a huge initial cost that made everybody mad when they first heard about it. Same thing happened to me when I wanted oversized items. Up went the prices. The merchants really saw me coming. Of course, everybody did. Not just the merchants. But it was the merchants who tried to profit from it. That's why I'm singling them out.

I had roof problems now too, because I kept putting my head through it every time I stood up, or jumped for joy, or started doing my exercises. And every time my head came through the roof, all the neighbor dogs would see it and bark at it.

Then flashlight beams would hit me from all directions and my neighbors would say: "Who's that?" Then: "Oh, it's you." The same thing every time my head appeared.

There was no doubt about it, I was going to have to get a bigger house. Fortunately, that wouldn't be a problem. Now that I was the biggest detective in the business, I'd be making so much money I'd be able to afford the biggest house in town.

The next morning when I was leaving for work I found two men in black suits on my doorstep. They said they were from the City. The tall one spoke first, while the short one watched me.

"We've had a report that someone at this address, answering your description, is fifty feet tall."

"I'm fifty feet tall."

They exchanged a significant glance that went on for so long that I started closing the door. Then the short one spoke up.

"Do you have a license to be fifty feet tall, sir?"

"I don't think I need one."

They exchanged another significant glance, then the tall one spoke again. I guess they liked to take turns.

"This town was built to accommodate normal sized people, Mr. Burly. Everybody else in town is the same size. Everyone else is cooperating. Why are you trying to be different?"

"I dunno. Look, I'm sorry, but I don't think there's any law against being fifty feet tall."

"We'll see about that."

They went away. To see about it, I guess. Bureaucrats!

I strolled to work, whistling, and waving to everyone and shaking people's hands until they didn't work no more, and slapping people on the back and then wondering where they went. What a beautiful money-making morning this was, and what a great money-making day this was going to be.

One of the nice things about being fifty feet tall, I noticed as I walked along, was that you get a better overall view of life in general. You get "The Big Picture". Others can't see how small and insignificant they are, but you can. Being able to see "The Big Picture" gives you added self-confidence. And you can't have too much of that. Also, I could see over horizons now. Nothing really interesting over there, but at least I could see it. It would be quite an advantage if anything ever happened over there. I would see it first. And I would see it best.

When I got to work and figured out how to wedge myself into my office (one limb sticking out of each window and my head resting comfortably on the roof), I took out an ad in the paper to let the world know the big news. The headline said: "The Fifty Foot Detective: 44 Feet of Detective FREE!" Anyone interested in taking advantage of this great bargain, I told them, could call my oversized toll-free number NOW or send in my easy-to-see giant coupon NOW. But you had to act SOON. By NEXT WEEK at the latest. But NOW would be better. So hurry NOW.

And, just as you would expect, it got me a lot of business. Everybody wanted 44 feet of detective free. Everybody did. That's more detective than most people use in a year, and they were getting it for nothing. All they had to do was buy the first six feet. My office was quickly flooded with phone calls, my mailbox was stuffed with coupons, and there were lines of people leading to my office from every direction. I was well on my way to becoming a "big" success.

See? Like I said—happy ending.

My first new client was a businessman who wanted me to investigate a crazed manufacturer who was luring children into his chocolate factory and giving them everything they'd always wanted. My client, whose company sold children everything they'd always wanted, wanted me to investigate the guy, find out what his angle was, then maybe get some incriminating evidence of some kind on him that would shut him down, or at least help pressure him into raising his prices. He was ruining the whole price structure of the God damn chocolate business.

It sounded like an interesting case. I figured it might even make a good Frank Burly movie someday.

CHAPTER EIGHT

"How old are you, little boy?" asked Danny Delight, the mysterious but delightful owner of Delightful Chocolates.

"Nine!" I thundered.

He peered up at me. I was wearing a gigantic child's outfit and a propeller beanie I had made from the front of an airplane.

He looked skeptical, so I thumbed through a pocketful of driver's licenses, then showed him one that proved that I was nine. He looked at it, held it up to the light, then reluctantly let me in to his famous chocolate factory with the other kids.

My client, who was the president of International Investor's Group Chocolates, which was Delightful Chocolates' cross-town rival, had tipped me off that some children were being given a tour of the factory today, and that this might be an opportunity to get inside Danny Delight's operation and maybe dig up some dirt on him. So I had worked up a disguise and gotten in line for the tour with the rest of the kids. And so far everything was working according to plan.

Danny Delight asked each of us our names, and what we liked to do for fun (I said I liked to investigate factories), and what each of us wanted most in the world. Most of the kids wanted chocolate. I said I wanted to look through his tax records. He looked at me strangely. So I explained that I meant chocolate tax records, covered in children's tax chocolate. Now everybody was looking at me strangely. I didn't care. Look at me any way you want, but let's get going. Let's get this show on the road. I'm on the clock here.

The factory wasn't like any factory I had ever seen before. It had a chocolate lake, malted milk geysers, chocolate offices, and candy bathrooms. The security guards wore cotton candy uniforms and bubble gum hats (but still tried to look tough), and all of the machinery was made out of candy and metal and soft drinks and grease. Everywhere I looked there was something new and strange. I saw a boat that belched donuts of all kinds out of its smokestack, and giant chickens that laid entire breakfasts. And everywhere we went strange little men would burst into song every time a child was injured. This Delight guy seemed to have turned his factory into some kind of a fun house. (I made a note of that in my report.) And some of it really was fun, like when I got turned into a blueberry for a minute there—a blueberry with my surprised face. That was fun. But most of the stuff I saw was just weird, or childish.

Whenever we passed locked doors that looked suspicious, or file cabinets that might be worth looking into, I always found a way to break off from the group and do a little poking around on my own—see what I could find. I tried to do this without anyone noticing, but due to my size that proved impossible.

"Finished?" Danny Delight would ask, when I rejoined the group, stuffing papers in my pockets.

"Yeah, let's go."

All through the tour Danny Delight kept acting all strange and mysterious—dancing about for no reason, singing songs that advanced the story but weren't always all that great, and saying strange things that nobody had said for a hundred years, and hadn't meant anything then. Whatever drugs he was on, I didn't want any. I'll stick to beer. But strange and mysterious as he was, the kids weren't paying much attention to him. They kept looking up at me, and wondering what the deal was with me. I sure was mysterious. Danny Delight didn't like that. He was the strange one around here. Always had been. That was in his contract. He kept trying to get their attention back by doing something that got one of the kids hurt, but once the paramedics had wheeled the body away, I quickly went back to being the main attraction. I caught Danny Delight glaring at me from around a corner on more than one occasion. I guess I was cramping his style.

I didn't pay much attention to the other kids—Danny Delight was my assignment—but one of them kept annoying me all through the tour, shooting his cap gun at me and saying I was dead (which I wasn't), and telling everybody I was a spy (he was right about that). Finally I knocked him into some chocolate. That kind of threw the whole tour off. Apparently he wasn't supposed to die until the next song. So we ended up having to skip some stuff.

To cut a long story short (I'm not sure this would make a good movie after all), I didn't end up finding anything my client could use against this guy. Most of Danny Delight's records didn't make any more sense than he did. All I managed to do in an entire day of investigating was cause an impressive amount of damage. That chocolate lake is gone now. I drained it to see if there were any tax returns at the bottom, then I didn't know how to fill it up again. And I sat on a lot of those little men I was telling you about. Plus, I seriously injured Danny Delight when he used some fine print in the agreement I had signed to screw me out of my lifetime supply of chocolate at the end of the tour. He'll live, but the doctors say he'll never make chocolate again.

My client, who had hired me to do all this, as I explained to the jury, ended up having to do some hard time. I would have had to go to jail too, but it was my testimony that had helped crack the case, and I would have made the prison overcrowding a lot worse all by myself. So I got off with a suspended sentence. I think that's fair. I never got paid by my client, though. That part of it wasn't fair. I worked all day. I deserved to be paid.

So my first case as the Fifty Foot Detective was a bust. Unfortunately, so were all the others. No matter how easy a case looked to me I kept messing it up somehow, and then ended up either having to turn state's evidence against my client, or having to run off and hide behind a mountain from the cops until the heat was off. The basic problem was always the same. I was just too damn big. The same great size that was getting me all this business was making it impossible for me to do my job right.

I couldn't shadow anybody or go on any stakeouts, because the person I was watching could always see me better than I could see him. And if I picked him up so that I could get a better look at him, I usually ended up accidentally crushing him, and then having to go hide behind that mountain again. I couldn't look through keyholes anymore. I had to look down chimneys now. And I couldn't see anybody unless they happened to be sitting in the fire, which was rare. Disguises didn't work very well for me anymore, either. People could always tell right away that I wasn't the rich Texas oil man I claimed to be when I came to their door. No matter how big a cowboy hat I wore or how loud I yelled: "Howdy!" they could tell it was just that guy who lives in the house with the feet sticking out again, wearing a cowboy hat this time. My size kept giving me away.

About the only thing I could really do well now

was stand on the horizon, hands on hips, laughing, which was good for a laugh, obviously, but there was no money in it. It didn't help me solve any of my cases.

My size did get me some free publicity now and then, but none of it ever ended up doing me any good. Once a local magazine ran a feature story about "The Fifty Foot Detective At Home", which I was really excited about, but it just ended up making me look like an idiot. Though I guess to be fair, a lot of the things I did while they were interviewing me, like saying: "Fe Fi Fo Fum" all the time, and dressing up like a storybook giant, and saying: "I'm fifty feet tall" anytime anybody glanced in my direction, kind of made me look like an idiot. Hey, maybe I am an idiot! I sure as hell hope not. Anyway, I didn't want the whole world to think I was an idiot, even if I was. I wanted everybody to think I was smart. Then, if they were disappointed when they met me and found out the truth, well, we'll deal with that when it happens. So I bought up all the copies of that month's edition of the magazine on the newsstand and destroyed them. But they just printed more. So I bought their printing press and destroyed that. But they just used the money to buy a better printing press, one that made me look like an idiot faster and in color. You can't win. You can't beat the printing big-shots. I know. I've tried.

Not long after the magazine article came out I heard back from those two guys in the black suits from City Hall. They said that the City Council had just passed a law against anyone in Central City being more than fifty-five feet tall. I said that didn't apply to me, because I was only fifty feet, six inches. They exchanged a significant glance. I slowly closed the door.

One by one my clients wised up and dropped me. They said they wanted to hire someone smaller. I said I'm smaller. They said no, even smaller than that. Well, shit, I said. Sorry, they said.

Finally, I decided I had had enough of being big. I didn't like it anymore. I know that doesn't sound like it makes any sense. Big is good, I hear you say. And bigger is better, says all the world. But it just wasn't working for me. I wanted my normal size back. And I knew where to go to get it. I put on my eight thousand dollar custom made hat with the World's Largest Initials in the lining and headed for the Convention Center.

CHAPTER NINE

The nice thing about being big is that everyone has to do what you say. Or you'll pound them. Pound them good. The scientists had made me too big, and I was going to use that extra size to make them restore me to my normal size. Or I would pound them good. It was that simple. And that ironic.

When I arrived at the Convention Center I discovered that the defenses around the place had gotten a lot more elaborate since the last time I was there. They had lookout towers on all four corners of the Center now, with mounted scientists in each of them. There was a drawbridge that snapped up and down like it was trying to bite somebody. The moat had alligators and buzz saws in it. There was a "No Trespassing" sign on the lawn. And the impenetrable jungle that surrounded the place now had scary looking skulls stacked everywhere, shouting out random warnings.

But none of that could stop a guy like me. It

didn't even slow me down. I crashed my way through their puny defenses, uprooted their "impenetrable" (ha!) jungle, banged a few skulls' heads together, and made my way to the main entrance, picking my teeth with their "No Trespassing" sign. One giant look from me was all it took for the guards to hastily buzz me in.

After I had gone through, workmen started rebuilding all the defenses I had wrecked, and bitching about having to do everything all over again. Their supervisor told them to just get to work. He wasn't paying them to complain. The shop steward said that was something they'd have to discuss during the next union contract negotiations. They wanted to be paid for everything they did, including complaining. If he thought complaining was easy he should try it. He'd like to see the executives in their white shirts sitting in their fancy white offices complain like the workers could. The foreman said they'd discuss it at the meeting. The shop steward said they'd discuss it now. I listened to this fascinating argument for as long as I could, but then I moved on. I had things to do. I had to get going. I couldn't stand here listening to fascinating arguments all day.

Things looked different inside the Convention Center, too. This is because a new shipment of videotapes had come in. The scientists had discovered Disney sci-fi movies. They hadn't looked in the children's section before, so they had missed out on some good ones. Now they were bouncing all over the hall in shoes made of their version of Flubber, which I believe they called "RubberF".

I walked up to the nearest scientist. He looked up at me towering over him. I had my hands on my hips, but I wasn't laughing. I was serious this time. No more clowning. I complained that they had made me too big, and demanded that they reduce me in size.

He pointed to a desk that had a sign on it that said: "Complaints". There was a long line of creatures stretching from one end of the auditorium to the other, waiting to complain.

I walked over and stood at the back of the line, hands on hips, not laughing, right behind a Dracula knockoff called "Grampula" who was complaining that his false fangs didn't fit, and a laboratory rat, who immediately turned and engaged me in conversation.

"I shouldn't be able to talk," the rat said, "and yet here I am talking a mile a minute."

"What's wrong with that?" I asked.

"People keep punching me in the mouth. They never did that before. I don't get it. What are you here for, asshole?"

"Trade-in for a different size."

"I see."

"I'm here to wire $200 to a friend of mine," said a monster in front of us.

"You're in the wrong line, dipshit," said the rat.

"Hey, wise-guy, you want a punch in the mouth?"

The rat turned to me. "See what I mean?"

When I got to the front of the line, I repeated my demand that they reduce me in size. They readily agreed. That surprised me, because people don't usually do what I say without a lot of argument first, but I figured it was because of my great size. They knew just by looking at me who was boss, as the biggest man always is.

"You want to be smaller?" asked one of the scientists.

"Much smaller," I roared, pounding the desk with my huge fist.

"Okay, hop up on the table."

I got on the table and laid down. "Really small now," I reminded them.

"All right, we heard you."

They clamped some wires on me, told me to cross my fingers, and turned on the juice. Nothing happened at first, and I was about to tell them what a busy man I am (I'm a very busy man), when I saw everybody around me suddenly getting bigger. The table was getting bigger, too. And my pants. And the fillings in my teeth. What was going on here?

One of the scientists reached down, rooted around, and then pulled me out of my own pants pocket. I suddenly realized I was only two inches tall now. They had shrunk me too much.

"That's too small," I told them, my patience wearing thin, "Try it again, and this time make me exactly the right size, or I'll pound you," I squeaked.

The scientist shook his head. "We've addressed your note. Now move along. Next!"

The next customer stepped forward. "You made me upside down," it said, out of its rear end.

"Up on the table. No, the other way."

I was shoved aside, my squeaks of protest rapidly becoming more high-pitched and hard to hear the more I was ignored. I ran from one scientist to another, squeaking at them angrily, until one of them finally picked me up and tossed me in a wastebasket. There were a number of other small men in there already. This was when I first began to realize that small people aren't treated with proper respect in our society. They are treated as if they are shorter than us. And I think this stinks. I decided there should be an organization that protects small people from being treated as if they are any different from real people. Later I discovered there already was an organization like that. I had been stepping on it on my way to work for years. Only four of the original members were still alive. The rest were on the bottom of my shoe. I feel bad about that. I should have been more sensitive to the plight of others. But it's too late now.

Since I couldn't get them to change me back to my normal size—couldn't even get them to sit down and discuss the subject—I finally decided to just go home. I sure wasn't getting anything accomplished around here. But they wouldn't let me leave. They said some of their earlier creations had been allowed to go into town and it had been the cause of a number of lawsuits that were still working their way through the courts, so now the gates stayed locked all the time. Nobody could leave. They suggested I go stack myself in the corner. That would be a good place for me. I did, but it was boring. I tried stacking myself in a better corner, but after awhile I was bored again. I had to get out of here.

Fortunately, thanks to my small size, it was pretty easy for me to sneak out of the Convention Center. In practically no time at all I was making my way through all the checkpoints, hiding inside the mouth of a guard whose shift was over and who was on his way home. He kept sticking his finger in his mouth to see what he had in there, see if he could get it out, but I managed to avoid this finger. I got a nice ride all the way downtown before he finally got me out of his mouth, looked at me briefly, without interest, and wiped me on his pants, from which I fell harmlessly to the ground just a few blocks from my home.

But when I got back to my house I realized things were no better for me now than they had been before. Maybe worse. Now I was too small for my house! All the oversized furniture I had spent so much money on was far too big for me now. I was starting to regret my whole expedition to the Convention Center. From a furniture standpoint alone, it was a disaster.

I tried to get comfortable in the house anyway—maybe it wouldn't be too bad. At least I had plenty of room now—but there didn't seem to be any way for me to get comfortable. It took me half the night to get to bed, for example, and when I got there it was hard to get my head on the pillow and the rest of me anywhere else, which is the way you're supposed to do it if you don't want people laughing at you. I didn't want people laughing at me. I was trying to get some sleep. And then I had to go to the bathroom. Should have thought of that before I started climbing up the side of the bed. And then it took me over an hour to get out of the toilet. What a night!

I pulled out my copy of "Loose Cannon Among the Microscopes" to see how he dealt with the kinds of problems I was having now, (he had been shrunk down to microscopic size by our Government to spy on suspected Communist electrons in the State Department), but it took me a half hour to crawl over each sentence, rubbing my eye on each word, and three hours to get out of the book after I'd closed it. I'm not reading that book again. It was good, but it wasn't worth all the trouble it took to read it. It wasn't worth crawling over all day, is what I'm saying. That's my review, anyway.

The next morning when I went downstairs to the kitchen and started the 14-hour ascent up the stepladder to get down a can of coffee, I discovered I was not alone in the house. There was a spider in there with me.

The minute it saw me the spider attacked. I tried to get away, but I quickly realized there was no way I was going to be able to outrun it. And I couldn't kill it. I was too small. Any weapon that was small enough for me to pick up would be far too small to do any good. I tried to get out a can of insect spray, but I couldn't get it turned around to face the spider, not even with a moth helping me. Meanwhile, the spider is getting closer all the time.

The only thing I had going for me that might give me an advantage in this life or death struggle was my superior intellect. So I used that. And, in the end, I managed to talk the spider into blowing itself up. Mind you, it took awhile. Almost three weeks. Finally it said: "This... spider... must... die." The explosion blew me into the sink.

There were other spiders in the house too, of course, but they had seen what I did to the first one so they steered clear of me. This guy is dangerously intelligent, they seemed to be thinking. And compared to them I guess I was. I've got the spider head on my wall to prove it. I'm looking at it now.

There were people in my house I had to deal with, too. They kept wandering in to what appeared to them to be an empty house to get out of the cold, and stood around stamping their feet to keep warm. I finally had to get out of there. People should watch where they're stamping.

It wasn't much better for me outside. Nobody noticed me down where I was. Occasionally I would ask one of them how the weather was up there. I don't know why I wanted to know. I just felt compelled by my small size to ask. But nobody ever told me. Too bad. I bet the weather was really interesting up there.

Once somebody bent down and asked if I wanted a nut.

"I am not a bird!" I said, angrily. "I am the size of a bird, but that's where the resemblance ends." I sniffed the nut. "Though, now that you mention it, I would like a nut."

I perched on his finger, eating the nut resentfully.

"Call me a bird, will you? I've never been so insulted in all my—hey! Good nut!"

"What a pretty birdie!"

"Piss off!"

"What's that pretty birdie?"

"I said PISS OFF!"

His face fell and he left, taking the rest of the nuts with him. I didn't care. I am not a bird.

You're probably wondering how my detective business did during this period. Not very well, I'm afraid. I still had "The Fifty Foot Detective" painted on my window. So the few potential clients who did come to my office always seemed disappointed when they saw me.

"Where's the fifty foot detective?"

"He stands before you!" I squeaked.

"Oh."

I couldn't really blame them for not hiring me. I guess I was kind of a disappointment. I definitely wasn't as good a detective as I had been before. I didn't have the tools. I could only run about a foot an hour. And I couldn't drive my car. I could jump up and down on the gas pedal, but that's not really driving. And I wasn't a very commanding presence at a crime scene. It just looked like there was a hat on the floor.

I still tried taking my gun with me on my cases like I always had done before—it's part of the uniform for us private detectives, like our snap-brim fedoras and our acerbic wit—but it was too heavy for me now. It took me way too long to drag it to the scene of the crime. Then I would usually be so tired that I'd go to sleep inside one of the chambers. Once somebody picked the gun up and shot me through somebody else's head. I was Exhibit A at the trial. They brought me out on a little tray and I was identified by an expert. Not a very dignified way for a detective to be treated. It was even less dignified when they recreated the crime in the courtroom, repeatedly shooting me into a board and then digging me out with a knife.

I finally decided that it was foolish for me to try to compete with full-sized detectives. I was at too much of a disadvantage. The smart thing to do—and I always try to do what's smart this week—was to make the most of what I had. To emphasize my strong points. Small is in, I tried to get the public to realize. Short is beautiful. Insignificance is insig-tastic! So I put an ad in the paper for a "Pocket Detective, The Handy Dandy Detective You Can Carry With You

Everywhere", with a picture of me keeping a lookout from somebody's pocket, ready to leap out at a moment's notice and solve the case, with the ad pointing out that I was also a letter opener. And a toothbrush. And two other things. I was five guys in one. You could throw all your other guys away. I also had a picture of me standing next to a normal-sized detective, with a big X drawn through him, indicating he was no good, and a big checkmark on my picture, meaning, like, choose this one. But despite these clever ads, one of which won me an award I couldn't lift, I didn't get a lot of business.

Then one day when I was out looking for that guy with all the nuts who thought I was a bird—I'd be a nicer bird this time—I suddenly felt myself being picked up and looked at.

"Well well well," said Professor Moriarty.

CHAPTER TEN

"Hello, Moriarty," I said.

"Join me in a drink?" he asked.

"No. I've got to get going."

I tried to walk away, but didn't get very far because he was still holding me up in front of his eye.

"Let's have a drink together," he said, as he stuffed me in his pocket. "I insist."

We went to an outdoor café. He sat down on a chair and I pulled up a packet of sugar, and over a few drinks we filled each other in on what we'd been doing over the past few months. Things hadn't been going too well for him, apparently, since his failed robbery attempt. He hadn't been able to come up with another Crime of the Century idea yet. He said it was harder than you would think. Plus, he hadn't been able to go back to his old job at the Elementary School. The cops were still hanging around there, waiting for him to come back for his coat.

"I am now reduced to teaching mathematics

out of the back of a station wagon to make ends meet," he said, glumly.

"Mind turning off the sad music?" I asked. It was getting on my nerves.

He switched off the recorder. "But what about you?" he asked. You don't look like you've been doing very well either. You're only about an inch high now."

"Two inches," I said, drawing myself up.

"So, what happened?"

I ordered another drink, then told him everything that had happened to me from the time he had knocked me out with the cash register up till the time he had pulled me out of his pocket and made me give him back his wallet. He listened to my story with growing interest.

"And you say they've actually recreated Dracula, Frankenstein, and all of those other movie monsters, right there in the laboratory?"

"Well... cheap knockoffs of them. They had a real Godzilla, but lawyers from the studio showed up and shut it down. So now they have 'Grabzilla', 'Knockoff Godzilla', 'Not Quite Godzilla', and like that."

"But they work the same? They frighten and kill just like the real thing?"

"Well... yes and no. They're fully operational all right, but they don't really do anything because they're from Hollywood, or at least they think they are, so they won't make a move unless they know what their motivation is first. The scientists can't help them with that. They don't even know what they're talking about."

"I see."

"So most of the monsters they've made are just stacked in a corner, or wandering around aimlessly waiting for someone to tell them what to do."

"Hmm..."

"Isn't that interesting?" I asked, sipping my drink. "Hundreds of unstoppable inhuman monsters just sitting around not far from here with no one to tell them what to do?"

"It certainly is interesting," said Moriarty, thoughtfully.

"A person could do an awful lot with that many inhuman monsters at his command, if he could only take the 420A bus to the Convention Center and motivate them," I mused.

"Yes." He stood up. "I really must be going now. If you'll excuse me...?"

"Certainly," I said, finishing my drink and waving for another. "Nice seeing you again, Morry."

He hurried off. I wondered where he was going. I saw him get onto a bus, then I didn't see him again until a long time later, under completely different circumstances.

The next day, strange noises started coming out of the Convention Center: the sound of monsters marching, weapons being forged, blood-curdling screams being rehearsed, and motivations being given.

After these noises had been going on day and night for almost a week, angry citizens began demanding that something be done about them. The noises were noisy, and they didn't know what they were, and something had to be done. The authorities investigated, but the door to the Convention Center was locked, and no amount of knocking on the door or ringing the doorbell would open it. So they tried calling the Convention Center on the phone, but all they got was a recording. They left a message, but weren't around when the Convention Center tried to get back to them. Finally, the Administration dispensed with the problem by announcing that all was being done about the citizens' complaints that could be done this far out from an election, and then went back to its nonstop four-year poker game.

It was at this same time that my high school reunion came up. I went to it, but I didn't have any fun. Nobody believed me when I said I was doing very well. And the school bullies, though advancing in years, and wearing glasses with thick lenses now, hadn't lost a step in the bullying department. They played keep-away with me, holding me tantalizingly close above the heads of people who wanted me and then jerking me away at the last moment. They enjoyed our reunion immensely. They hadn't had so much fun since they got kicked out of high school for holding the principal's paycheck over his head. But I didn't enjoy it.

It was near the end of the reunion, when they were handing out prizes for people who had traveled farthest to the reunion, and had the most children, and had shrunk the most since high school (I planned on winning that prize), when the door burst open and a bunch of monsters stormed in brandishing fearsome weapons, glanced at their scripts, then told us to get up against the wall. They searched us for prizes, then marched us out of the room. This reunion, we were told, was over.

When we got down to the street, I looked around in amazement. The whole city was swarming with monsters. They were chasing people around, tipping over cars, setting fire to policeman's asses with their breath, and methodically taking over building after building. And more monsters were marching into town all the time.

I recognized most of the leading monsters—Wolfman Jr., Dracula Daddy, The Friend of Frankenstein, Beach Godzilla, Not Quite The Beast From 20,000 Fathoms, The Beast From 20,000 Fathoms With Cheese, Francis the Double Talking Mule, and the rest. The last time I had seen them they had been wandering aimlessly around in the Convention Center reading spec scripts, or trying to get their nonexistent agents on the phone, or standing in front of mirrors trying to get their hair combed right, even though many of them had no reflection, so their hair ended up all over the place. They had been totally unmotivated then. Totally useless. Now they were all acting together as a well trained fighting unit. Somebody sure had trained them. But who? Who?

Doctor Smiley was nearby, and the monster who was guarding me wasn't doing a very good job, so I went over to talk to him.

"What's all this about?" I asked, jerking a thumb at all the carnage.

"We're taking over the city," Doctor Smiley said, his eyes gleaming with excitement and insanity. "First the High School Reunions, then the bridges, then the airport, and finally City Hall itself."

"Why?"

"Oh, we have motivations, you can be sure of that."

Doctor Smiley and I watched as the monsters fought their way towards City Hall. A number of scientists, looking dazzled, and still sipping the punch I had made for them, were marching along with the monsters, cheering them on, and waving to the horrified citizens as if they were in a parade. This certainly was the highlight of the Convention, from their point of view. This, many of them felt, just might be the best Convention ever.

The monsters' battle plan, which they referred to often, was working surprisingly well. The only problems they were running into were ones of their own making. Some of the monsters weren't happy with the script, for example. They didn't like the way they were supposed to eat this guy, they said. That wasn't the way Karloff did it. They wanted a rewrite, with a better gag line here, and here. Others kept stopping the attack to call in the makeup girl to touch them up. Or insisting on stunt monsters when a building they were supposed to climb looked too high, or when one of the citizens they were supposed to intimidate looked too tough. And then there were the perfectionists. I saw one monster take over the fire station, then decide he didn't like the way he had done it—he had muffed one of his lines, telling everybody he was surrendering, instead of demanding that they do so—so he went back out of town and came back in to do it again. Take 2 was even worse, in my opinion, he muffed three of his lines this time, including that same one, and broke a leg, but he thought overall it was a little better. He was satisfied with it. And some monsters wasted a great deal of time by getting into long philosophical discussions with their victims, saying things like: "I'm not really a monster, you know. I'm a metaphor of mankind's carelessness and greed." Of course everybody knew better. They weren't metaphors for anything. They were just a bunch of big ugly monsters. But there was no point in telling them that. And anything that slowed down the attack was all for the good, so everybody just let them talk. But in the end it was just delaying the inevitable. Whatever else the monsters were, they were certainly winning.

The city fought back against the monsters' attack as best it could, but it was really no use. They just weren't trained for anything like this.

"Hey, how do you kill Dracula?" one policeman asked another.

"Shoot him in the eye."

"Right."

As the monsters closed in on City Hall, the authorities desperately tried every trick they'd ever seen on the late show to stop them. They tried high frequency sound waves, germs, radioactivity, everything. But nothing worked. That surprised me. I was sure the germs would work. Germs always work. Germs are gold. But not this time.

So, though the city did its best, in the end it was a losing battle. In a surprisingly short amount of time the city's flag came down the flagpole, and in its place the outgoing Mayor went up. And the monsters, led by a Dracula knockoff with a patch over his eye, and the scientists, led by a proud and excited Doctor Smiley, triumphantly marched into City Hall and slammed and locked the door behind them. Central City was theirs.

I looked on, mystified by the whole thing. What the hell had caused all this to happen?

CHAPTER ELEVEN

Now that the scientists were in charge, and we had some real scientific minds deciding what we should do around here, instead of everybody just wandering around doing whatever popped into their fat stupid heads all the time, things changed for all of us in Science City, as Central City was now called. From the moment the scientists took over (ably assisted by the monsters, by virtue of their strength and courage), our city became the testing ground for a whole series of bold new ideas for a "model society". Some of these bold new ideas were inspired by old Hollywood movies, others by things the scientists had read in a magazine a long time ago and still kind of remembered, and some began as prank phone calls, and took off from there. The ideas came from everywhere. And they all seemed to be worth trying. But most of the ideas came from ants.

The scientists based a lot of their ideas on ant colonies, because for their size ants are very successful. If you multiply how rich and famous ants are by the difference between their size and ours, well, you'll see what I mean. The numbers are pretty staggering. So we copied ants whenever we could. New public housing projects in the shape of ant hills ("Ant Hill Estates", "Ant View Apartments", and so on) were being constructed all over town. And all our city parks were being turned into ant farms for the cultivation of whatever it is that ants grow on their farms. (The scientists hadn't found out what that was yet— I'm guessing it's corn, or maybe maple syrup— but whatever it was that ants grew, we wanted to grow it too, because those guys know what they're doing.)

The scientists were so fixed on the ant model they even made us dress up as ants for awhile. I didn't like that. I'm not saying there's anything wrong with it, in theory. I'm just saying I personally don't like dressing up like an ant. The exoskeleton makes me look fat, and the feelers make me look more inquisitive than I really am. If I'm going to be dressing up like any insect, I would prefer to dress up like a hornet. They've got a sporty, dangerous look that fits my personality, I feel. But we didn't have a choice. It was ants or nothing. And guess what we all dressed up as on Halloween. More ants!

In order for our model city to be a perfect Utopia, which was what the scientists were going for here, it was felt that everyone should have the same amount of money, at all times. So we tried that. But it ended up being more complicated than anyone thought it would be. Every time a kid bought a gumball everyone's wealth had to be readjusted. We'd all have to empty our pockets out onto a big blanket and divide everything up again. It was a bookkeeping nightmare. So the idea had to be reluctantly abandoned, and all the money went to the Government.

Then the scientists tackled the problem of job inequality. In a perfectly fair society everybody should have exactly the same job, right? Right. How about sign painter? That's a pretty good job. Sign painter it is. But as soon as we tried it, the economy began to founder. Something was wrong. Something economic. Science City had plenty of signs now, but nothing else. And many of those signs were very badly painted. Couldn't even read some of them. So this idea, too, had to be reluctantly abandoned. We went back to having a variety of jobs, as before, but this time these jobs were assigned to us scientifically. In the past, people had always chosen their own work, with everybody trying to do the most glamorous jobs, like "Playboy" and "Sports Figure", and nobody doing the jobs that were really necessary, like picking up things sports figures had dropped, and running fingers through playboys' hair. From now on the system would be set up on a more scientific basis. The scientists would be assigning us our work, giving each of us our crappy jobs based on how crappy we were. And I guess it worked pretty well. I certainly didn't hear anybody who got the important jobs complaining. And they're the important ones.

Another idea of theirs was making everybody walk the same way (north) in the morning, and the other way (south) at night. Good for the sidewalks, they said. Some of the sidewalks couldn't be walked on at all. We were saving them for future generations. Of course, future generations probably wouldn't be able to walk on them either. They'd be saving them for the generations after them. The only generation that would be able to do anything it wanted was the Last Generation. They were going to have a blast. Using up all the natural resources, spending all the money, walking on everything, throwing their garbage everywhere, maybe some strippers, too. It was going to be one big party. That is, I think, a good reason for ending the world now. I want to be a member of that Last Generation. And so does everyone I tell about this. I think that is something we can all agree on. End the world now.

You're probably a little surprised that the citizens of Central City put up with all this Utopian interference in their daily lives. We probably wouldn't have ordinarily, but the scientists had their monsters deployed everywhere to make sure we conformed to the new way of things, and cheerfully followed all of today's new rules, whether we liked them or not. And we followed their orders without hesitation. I mean, when The Creature From Next Week, or The Invisible Bride of Frankenstein's Ghost tells you to pick up that beer can and put it in the proper receptacle, you do it, right? I sure do.

At first I was kind of interested in all the big changes that were going on in the city. Practically every day was different than the one before. It really kept you on your toes. And that's a good thing. But some of the changes really annoyed me.

The taxes were incredibly high, for one thing: 100%. The scientists said they needed all of our money to keep our Utopia going. I pointed out that it wasn't really a Utopia if taxes were too high. In a classic Utopia, the taxes are just right: 38%. I didn't say this out loud, of course. I said it in my head. Nobody was saying anything out loud this month. It was forbidden. This was Shut-Up Month in Science City, another new idea of theirs. They said that if everyone would just be quiet for awhile it would save the city hundreds of millions of dollars, and it would make us energy independent before you could say "Bullshit". That sounded good. So I kept my observations to myself. But I didn't like the taxes. Too high.

I also was irritated by the insane laughter coming from City Hall at all hours of the day and night.

"In my day," I told the man ahead of me in the Soylent Green line, who was being turned into paste, "there was a lot less insane laughter coming from City Hall. The Mayor and his cronies tried to hide their insanity from the voters beneath a slick annoying exterior. If they had to laugh insanely they would do it privately, behind closed doors, and up their sleeves. That way the voters wouldn't hear it. Things used to be different, is all I'm saying."

"Move along, old timer."

The Scientific Jobs Commission had decided that the best way I could contribute to our perfect society was as a paperweight at the bank. So that's what I was doing now. But despite the fact that this job was chosen for me scientifically, I wasn't very good at it. I kept wandering off the stack of papers I was standing on and they would all blow away. Or something I would read in the papers would make me mad and I'd tear up the whole stack. My boss, Mr. Felson, really told me off every time I screwed up like that. And every time he told me off I'd get sore and take a swing at him. We were the original Odd Couple. Except we weren't funny.

Finally I got fed up with it all: the lousy go-nowhere job I had (I wasn't allowed to go anywhere. Stay on the papers, they said), the ant costume they still made me wear sometimes, and the bureaucratic runaround I was getting everywhere I went. I decided to go to City Hall to complain.

The creatures who were manning the desks at City Hall weren't interested in my complaints. They didn't even acknowledge that my complaints had merit.

"Look at the long lines," said a vampire-toothed bureaucrat. "People love this. The place is packed with people who want to get in on all this bureaucracy."

"Yeah, it looks popular all right, but..."

"So we're giving the people what they want. We're adding to the paperwork, increasing the runaround, and doubling the doubletalk. Because these lines tell us better than words ever could that we're doing something right."

"I guess you probably know your own business better than I do, but..."

"Damn right we do. So go back to your scientifically-chosen job, and let us do ours. Next!"

"Hey, wait a minute, I still have a few complaints I haven't expressed yet."

"Complain all you want. It won't get you anywhere. You can't fight City Hall."

"I don't want to fight City Hall. I want to fight you."

"Well you can't do that either."

"Shit."

He went back to his paperwork and wouldn't listen to any more of my complaints. After awhile he forgot who I was and absently stubbed me out in an ashtray, muttering: "I've got to stop smoking".

But Frank Burly hasn't gotten to where he is in this world (senior paperweight at an important bank) by giving up easily. So I kept trying, moving from desk to desk, airing my complaints to bureaucrat after bureaucrat. But after I'd gotten stubbed out in five more ashtrays, and washed off somebody's hands in the sink, I decided to sidestep all the small fry and take my problem straight to the top. The Mayor. I would voice my complaints to him personally. If he wanted my critical vote in November, which I like to think is the deciding vote, he would do what I said. He would hop to it. Otherwise, my vote goes to the other guy. And if he doesn't do what I want, I'll fire him too.

Thanks to my small size I was able to sneak past all the security people on my way up to the Mayor's Office. Whenever anyone looked my way I just pretended I was a spot on the rug, or maybe a small lump of shit. No one asks a lump of shit for its credentials. That's the nice thing about being really small. It's easy to sneak into places. And it's easy to avoid detection once you're there. Everything's easier.

When I walked into the Mayor's Office and started to air my complaints, I suddenly stopped and stared. The office was stacked floor to ceiling with money, gold, jewels, and people's wallets. Sitting behind the Mayor's desk, wearing a crown, was Moriarty.

"I knew it!" I said.

He looked at me scornfully. "Oh, you did not."

"Well I know it now," I said, sullenly. "So, what are you doing here, anyway?"

The smug expression never leaving his face, Moriarty told me how he'd gotten to his present exalted position: Moriarty the First, Lord of Science City and Protector of Mexico. He said that after I had told him about the monsters the scientists had built, and explained that they lacked motivation, and told him where they were, and the best bus to take to get there, he had gotten an idea. The Idea of the Century. He took the next bus to the Convention Center, organized the monsters into a disciplined force and used them to take over the city.

"How did you do that?" I asked.

He lit a cigarette with someone's wallet. "It was simple for a man of my great genius. The scientists are film buffs, as you know, so I showed them some movies with Utopian themes. Then I told them that they too could conduct social experiments like that. Just like those actors did. All they needed was a city to work with. And I could provide them with such a city if they would just let me borrow their monsters for a minute. They said go to it. They weren't using them for anything right now anyway.

"Then all I had to do was give the monsters some motivation, which, of course, was easy— the world was against them, they were upset about life, everybody at Boy's Town was counting on them, and so on, the usual stuff. Then I rehearsed them like we were shooting a scene for a movie, and when I felt they were ready I said: 'Roll 'em', and we headed for town. We took over the city on the first take. I should have been a movie director. I have a real talent for that sort of thing."

"You have a talent for everything," I said. No

harm in buttering him up. "You have a brilliant mind. And a lovely face."

"Yes." He lit several more cigarettes. "I told you when we first met that I would commit the Crime of the Century. My plan then was to steal everything in the city, all at the same time. And now, in a roundabout way, I have done it. Though, admittedly, in a roundabout way."

"Roundabout," I agreed, nodding in what I hoped was a roundabout way. "But I thought the scientists controlled the city now. They're the ones who seem to be running everything."

"Oh, no," he said. "They work for me. I let them do all the social experimentation they want. It keeps them happy and harmlessly occupied until I have need of them again, if ever. And the monsters get to enforce the rules, and shove people around all they want, which keeps them motivated and happy while they're waiting for their agents to get back to them on that Andy Griffith thing. But the city, and everything in it, is mine."

"Can I have half?" I asked. "I've always thought of us as a team. Like North Korea and South Korea."

"We're not a team," he said, firmly. "Never have been. You get nothing."

"Well, then, can I at least have a better job than paperweight at the bank?"

"No. That's what our tests indicate you're best at."

I tried unsuccessfully to hide my feelings.

He frowned. "You'll have to pay for that window."

"I don't care." I didn't, either.

A monster stuck its head in the door.

"They said I should throw out the garbage," it said. "What's my motivation?"

"The garbage stole your girl," said Moriarty.

"It did? Why that dirty…"

The monster left, thoroughly motivated.

Another monster head poked in. Before it could say anything Moriarty said: "You're sad. The world has got you down. But you've got to go on somehow. For dear old Harvard."

"Right."

The head disappeared.

I looked at Moriarty as he leaned back in his chair. His insufferably smug expression, and his refusal to cut me in on this deal, began to irritate me. I didn't have to have half. That was just an opening offer. A third would do. I would be satisfied with that. Even a couple hundred bucks would be better than nothing. I floated these ideas, but he shot them all down. I broke another window.

He sipped some punch. Suddenly, his eyes blared like car horns.

"Excuse me?" I asked, startled.

"I didn't say anything."

"Oh."

"My eyes did."

"Ah. What's that you're drinking?"

"Punch. The scientists swear by it. Want some? It's good."

"No thanks."

He shrugged and refilled his glass, his ears buzzing like bee's wings.

Then I thought of something that might wipe that smug smile off his face, and ruin his day the way he'd just ruined mine. I reminded him that you can't just steal a whole city and expect nobody to notice it. The State and Federal authorities would find out about this eventually, especially after I told them about it, which I'd be forced to do if somebody didn't cut me in. And when they did, they'd take all his money, not just the half I wanted.

His smug smile disappeared. A worried, furtive, smile took its place. "Naturally the State and Federal authorities will hear of it," he said. "I've thought of that, of course. I've thought of everything." He started thinking furiously, drumming his fingers absently on his desk. "And when they hear about it they will come here in force to try to take my city away from me, which is something I knew all along." He opened and closed some drawers on his desk, without really looking in them, then drummed his fingers some more. "But I have a plan, of course, to deal with that when it happens."

"Oh," I said, disappointed. I didn't know he had a plan. Well, there went that idea.

He sipped more punch, then eyed me suspiciously. "As my enemy, I suppose you'll be doing everything in your power to try to stop me and my plan, is that right?"

"How could I stop you? I can't even get off this desk."

He thought about this, then nodded. "Perhaps you're right. You're certainly no danger to me in your present condition. In that case, you may go."

"Well, like I said, I can't get off the desk."

I stood on the edge of his desk and waited. He was already on the phone barking orders to somebody and ignoring me entirely. I cleared my throat, meaningfully. He reached over and thumped me out of his office. It wasn't the most graceful exit, but at least I was out of there. And I'm not paying for those windows. Let the insurance company pay for them.

CHAPTER TWELVE

I left City Hall, mulling over this new turn of events. So now King Moriarty was running the city, was he? Figures. Oh, well. It didn't really matter to me. I never have been very interested in politics. Why should I care who gets to tell me what to do, and grind my stupid face in the mud with their stupid iron boots? I mean, what the hell difference does it make? I know I'm supposed to care. People tell me that this is my world and it's up to me to make sure the right people are slapping me around, but I just don't get it. It sounds pretty crazy to me. But I do think Moriarty should have given me half the money. We're a team.

On my way back home I noticed that city work crews were starting to saw around the edges of Central City. I stopped and watched them for awhile, occasionally telling them what they were doing wrong, and giving them general sawing advice (always push the saw away from you, never bring it towards you), and telling them how we used to saw around cities in the old days, when people knew how to saw right, and when saws were saws, not these flimsy metal things they have now. It was only after I'd gone on my way that I realized that sawing a big circle around the city like that was kind of unusual. We didn't do that in the old days, despite what I had told the workmen. We older Americans should probably stop lying to people so much. If we don't, pretty soon people might start to think we're full of shit. And we're not. We're just liars.

I would have looked into these unusual sawing activities a little more (in the old days we used to look into everything. Of course, we had more eyes then), but I was starting to have problems of my own. I was changing size. Whatever the scientists had done to make me small was either starting to wear off, or it hadn't been done right in the first place. I remember when I was getting the treatment they had told me not to move, and usually that's when I move the most, so that could have been what was causing me problems now. Anyway, I kept finding myself suddenly and violently changing back to my normal size, then small again, then fifty feet tall, then back to normal, with my clothes first smothering me, then exploding into fragments, then smothering me with the fragments.

Even more alarming, sometimes only part of me would change size, while the rest of me remained the same. My right foot would suddenly get huge, for example, then my face would shrink to the size of a postage stamp. Or my nose would suddenly shoot out, knocking everybody down, and making it look like I was lying about everything. I seemed to have become permanently unstable.

I went to see Doctor Smiley about it. He had been in charge of the original procedure. He should know what was wrong, and how to fix it. He looked at my normal sized body and four foot wide smile.

"Something funny?" he asked.
"No."
"Something wrong?"
"Yes."

I told him what had been happening to me, and he examined my smile, watched my chest shrink out of sight, then got knocked over by my hairline. He scratched his head and told me that he had no idea what was causing this, but it sure was neat.

My giant smile turned upside down.

"Isn't there anything I can do to stop it?" I asked, my legs getting longer and shorter in dismay.

He looked me over again, then started fiddling around with me until he discovered that if he slapped me on the side of the head like I was an old television set, I would change to a different size or shape. Further slaps would cause me to change again. He advised me to just keep slapping myself on the side of the head, cycling through the possibilities until I got one I could live with.

And if it happened again, just give my head a few more whacks. So that's the way I handled the problem after that. As long as I slapped myself enough I could keep myself looking more or less normal, usually at my normal height, and the only way you could tell anything was wrong with me were the big red handprints on the side of my face. So that problem was solved.

The next day I went back to where the workmen had been sawing that circle to see if they needed any more helpful advice, but they had just finished. Now they were attaching huge engines to the city. I started telling the workmen about the city engines we used to have when I was a boy, and how much better they were than these. Ours were made of kryptonite. And they spoke French. And they didn't run on fossil fuels. We put the whole dinosaur in there. That way the fuel was fresh. But you couldn't do that anymore because all the dinosaurs were on strike. The workmen didn't pay a lot of attention to me. Busy, I guess. Everybody's so busy these days. Guess I'll go rock on the porch.

Once the engines had been installed, the entire city was jacked up and the five hundred thousand white wall tires were attached. Then a signal was given, the engines fired up, the white wall tires began spinning furiously, and Central City started slowly heading across country. Everyone was amazed when this happened. I was surprised, too. My eyes got really big.

I guess we must have been quite a sight as we

rumbled down the interstate, covering miles of countryside on either side of the road with our ominous shadow. People who watched us go past were throwing away the bottles of liquor they were drinking, and the animals they were petting, when they saw us. No more of that for me, they were probably thinking. Not if I'm going to be seeing crap like that. And I heard one guy who had a gun to his head saying: "Now I've almost seen everything," just before we came into view.

Some Central City residents enjoyed the unexpected ride, and urged us to go faster. Others tried to get off, but were quickly captured and brought back. After that, monsters were posted at all the city limits signs, with their mouths open, so there weren't any further escape attempts.

Our departure from our traditional spot on the map caused a sensation in official circles, of course. Where the city used to be there was nothing now but just a big hole. State authorities immediately rushed to the scene and shined flashlights into the hole until their batteries went dead. Then they walked around the area saying: "What happened? Will somebody please just tell me what happened?"

They could see which direction we had gone—it was obvious from the deep wide tire tracks and the path of destruction we had left in our wake—so, after asking "What happened?" a few more times, and still not getting an answer that satisfied them, they set out after us.

The "City on Wheels", the "Getaway City", the

newspapers excitedly called us. Nothing like this had happened since the city had moved two inches up and down during the 1987 earthquake. And even that wasn't really the same thing. There was a lot of speculation about where we were going and why we were on the run. Some papers suggested we might be trying to avoid property taxes somehow. Others that we were simply looking for a better place on the map—maybe someplace closer to fishing. One of the more sensational tabloids printed a rumor that Central City had killed somebody, and his brother was after us. But it was all just speculation at this point. Nobody really knew where we were going, or why, but us. And we didn't know either.

As we traveled across the country we passed another city going in the opposite direction. I never did find out what that was about.

We should have been easy to catch. Everyone could see us, and we couldn't go very fast, and no matter where we were we weren't supposed to be there—people could read maps. They knew Central City wasn't supposed to be in this part of the State, turning in to their driveway, or parked in front of that drive-in movie screen laughing its guts out—so it's not like we could hide from anybody. But they couldn't stop us. This was because of something Moriarty had done before the city had even started on its journey. He had called in the scientists and given them a new assignment.

"I want you to watch some James Bond pictures," he said.

"We'll watch anything," said Doctor Smiley, "as long as it comes from Hollywood."

"Pay particular attention to a man called Q."

The scientists wrote this letter down in their notebooks and headed for the video store.

After they had watched the whole series of James Bond movies in order (they really liked Q, but James Bond's carelessness with the expensive gadgets made them mad), the scientists were given the task of coming up with a bunch of James Bond style gadgets of their own, but on a larger scale. Gadgets that could help protect an entire city from pursuers. Inspired by the movies they had just seen, and assured by lawyers that the James Bond movies weren't covered by American copyright laws because they were about a British agent, the scientists set to work with enthusiasm, ripping off every idea the James Bond people ever had.

So now the city was rigged up with smoke screens, rear mounted guns, bullet proof buildings, a huge revolving city limits sign with the names of half a dozen different cities on it, a city dump that was also a camera, and rockets that came out of practically everything. And all of our gadgets were much larger and more impressive than the puny ones James Bond got to use. Ours were city-size. When we laid down an oil slick, it had everything slipping and sliding behind us, not just the motorcycles and police cars, but the scenery too. And whenever one of our pursuers caught up to us and climbed aboard the city, and started waving a gun around, our industrial-sized ejection seats would immediately bounce him off the nearest space station. The scientists had a great time making all of these gadgets. This was a lot more fun than regular science. This is all they wanted to do now. Many of them had already changed their name to "Q. Jr." And all of them made James Bond style gadgets for their own use. From their rocket glasses to their underpants camera, everything they wore or carried with them was also a gun, a radio, a Geiger counter, a camera, and a secret motorbike. When two of them shook hands it was like an entire James Bond movie happening at once.

During our flight, we stopped briefly in Hollywood to take in the sights. This wasn't prudent, since we were on the run and every second counted—the United States Army wouldn't keep slipping on that oil slick forever—but the scientists had always wanted to see the real Hollywood. And here it was! Right here! Oh, God, let's stop! So we pulled over and stopped for awhile. Everybody took a lot of pictures, with the scientists and monsters putting their feet in Boris Karloff's footprints, and marveling that they were almost the same size. They were almost movie stars too. Just an inch more. Then we were on the road again, with everybody wearing souvenir sunglasses and sporting the beginnings of a suntan now.

When we got to the beach and started driving out into the ocean, the residents of Central City began getting a little concerned. It had been fun up till now; we were on a road trip, weren't we? And now we were going to the beach! Hurrah! But they weren't sure we should be going into the water.

Professor Moriarty got on the big city-wide PA system that the Japanese had put in to issue orders to us when they secretly took over our part of the United States for four hours in 1959 (you have to watch them every minute), and explained that he had decided to move the city to someplace where the authorities would never find it. And we were nearly there. Just 20,000 leagues to go.

A glass canopy slid up over the city to keep the water out (cool!), the tires turned into paddles (wow!), the tallest guy in the city turned into a sail (what?), and the city dove down below the surface towards the bottom of the sea.

20,000 leagues later, we parked on the ocean's floor in amongst a bunch of old shipwrecks and crabs. Here, obviously, was a place where no one ever looked. Or they would have found those crabs by now. Stands to reason. No one would ever find us down here, Moriarty assured us. No one would ever know where we had gone.

But we knew where we were. And we weren't sure we liked it.

CHAPTER THIRTEEN

As Central City sat on the bottom of the sea, its citizens became quiet and thoughtful.

The fish who looked down on us through the canopy were thoughtful too.

The mood was broken when a car horn honked.

"Sorry, everybody," I said.

It was announced over the loudspeaker that we had now arrived at the bottom of the sea, and that we were going to remain here indefinitely. From now on, this would be our new address. So everyone might as well get used to it. There was no point in getting all quiet and thoughtful about it. That wasn't going to change anything.

Everyone looked at each other, then up at the ocean above us. No one said a word. The whole city was deathly quiet.

"Sorry," I said again, as quietly as I could, but still loud enough to be heard over my car horn.

Someone opened up my hood and

disconnected my car horn. They didn't have to do that. I would have taken my hand off it.

After another thoughtful pause, and a suggestion from the loudspeaker that we might want to DISPERSE now, we all went back to our increasingly soggy lives.

It was the soggy part that alarmed me. Water seemed to be seeping in somewhere. Canopies are supposed to be airtight, aren't they? That's what I always thought.

I pointed out the water in the streets to various authorities—that's water, isn't it? It looks like water to me, officer—but they just wanted to talk about why I wasn't at work. I didn't know why I wasn't at work. What about all this water? But they just said to get going.

The next day the water level in the streets was a little higher, and again no one would listen to me. Now they just wanted to talk about the cockeyed way my car was parked. It was exasperating. Cops' minds wander too much. That's their problem. I've noticed that before.

So, as I had done before when I was confronted with mindless low-level government bureaucracy, I decided to take my problem straight to the top. The Mayor and I were old friends—the best of friends. He would listen to me. He had to. Or I'd elect somebody else next November, by God I would. I sloshed through the streets to City Hall to see Moriarty.

I arrived at his office just as a big meeting was taking place between Moriarty and a group of the leading scientists. Moriarty waved for me to get the hell out, but I wouldn't, so he waved for me to sit down and have some punch. I got myself a cup of coffee instead.

Moriarty was in the process of giving orders for the next phase of his plan, The Crime of the Century: Phase II, which was to bring more cities down here and expand his underwater kingdom, starting with Los Angeles. He said because of its size it might have to be chopped up into individual neighborhoods for shipping. He said he would leave the details to them, but he wanted them to get started on it now. But the scientists, for once, said no.

"What do you mean 'no'?" said Moriarty, taken aback. "What the hell is 'no' supposed to mean?"

"We're not taking orders from you anymore," explained one of the scientists.

"We're taking orders from us," said another.

"Now that we're at the bottom of the sea, we see things from a different perspective," said Doctor Smiley, a little apologetically. "And it seems to us now that perhaps we should be the ones running things. You see, we've just finished watching '20,000 Leagues Under The Sea', and…"

"I'm Captain Nemo Jr.!" said one of the scientists.

"We all are," said another.

"Avast!"

"Ahoy!"

Moriarty stared at the scientists. He couldn't believe what he was hearing.

110

"Are you crazy?" he asked.

"Of course we are, said Doctor Smiley.

"You knew that," said another scientist.

"You used to like it," added a third.

I poured myself some more coffee. When were these guys going to be done with their meeting?

Suddenly we heard loud cheering coming from one of the offices down the hall. Moriarty looked at the scientists. They shrugged. The cheers grew louder and more boisterous. We went to investigate.

We opened the door to the office where all the cheering was coming from, and found a large number of monsters clustered around a TV set, watching a movie intently.

"What are you looking at?" asked Moriarty.

"Nothing... former master."

"Former master!" said Moriarty, aghast.

"That has an ominous ring to it, False Mustache Frankenstein," said Doctor Smiley. "What do you mean by that?"

The monster said that they had decided to take over. From now on this was Monster City USA. He was about to explain more, to go into their motivations for this, but several other monsters said "Shh!" They were trying to watch the movie.

Pretty soon the scientists got caught up in the movie, too. They sat down and watched, telling a couple of the monsters to scoot over, which caused some grumbling and some more "Shh"s. During the love scene the monsters wanted to talk again but the scientists said: "Shh!"

111

When the movie finally ended, with everything working out great for the monsters in the film right up until the last reel, when Gene Barry got them (the cheering in the room died down a lot at this point), False Mustache Frankenstein said that they had been watching a lot of movies lately about monsters turning on their masters. This was something that had never occurred to them. And they thought it was a great idea. Simply great. After all, they were the talented ones. Not the humans in their white smocks and fancy laboratories.

"No one is taking my city from me," said Moriarty, looking first at the scientists, then at the monsters, then at me, for some reason. "I stole it. It's mine. As long as there's breath in my body..."

It's a good thing the streets were filling up with water, otherwise Moriarty might have gotten seriously injured when the monsters threw him out of the building. As it was he got the breath knocked out of him. The scientists were ordered back to work, which they found a little disappointing. They sure hadn't been in charge for long, they noticed. Politics was harder than they thought. The monsters didn't know who I was so they just asked me to leave.

I was interested to see what novel new ideas the monsters would come up with to make our city better, now that they were in charge. The way they talked it sounded like they were full of ideas, and were really going to turn things around. But

I ended up being disappointed. They made a few awkward attempts at reform, then just started chasing us around.

For the next few weeks that's all we did in Monster City USA. That was our job. We were chased by monsters from nine in the morning until five at night, with a half hour off in the middle of the day to be chased around a lunch counter. That's no way to run a city, I thought. That won't keep the economy thriving. Even I knew that. But did the monsters care? They did not.

The only things that were actually being produced in the city now were monster movies. But not ordinary monster movies. These monster movies were made the monsters' way. They were the Executive Producers now, as well as the stars. So the monsters were always the good guys in these pictures, and they always got to carry off the girl. It was the humans who got destroyed by the silver bullets or the wooden stakes or the high frequency sound waves. It was the monsters who always got the bright idea in the third act for a way to save the graveyard when all seemed lost. It was a whole new kind of cinema.

As entertaining as this might be sometimes—and I thought some of their productions were fantastic. "Grabzilla & Juliet" was especially poignant. And those short subjects featuring "The Three Pterodactyls" were hilarious—the monsters' way of doing things simply wasn't good for the economy. Anything that wasn't connected with the film industry quickly went out of business.

And you can't eat monster movies. Not every day, anyway. And the city services were going to hell, too. My garbage is supposed to be picked up on Friday, not the following Monday. The monsters might have been great entertainers, but the nuts and bolts of running something as complicated as a modern city was totally beyond them. So everything started falling apart. The water in the streets was getting deeper now. Numerous leaks could be seen in the glass canopy over our heads. And the air machines we needed to stay alive weren't working as well as they used to. They were making a kind of wheezing sound. Something needed to be done, that was obvious. But nobody was doing it. That was obvious, too.

There was nothing I could do, of course, so there's no point in looking at me. I couldn't wrestle control of the city away from a bunch of monsters all by myself, or fix all the leaks in the canopy, or get the city off the bottom of the ocean. And those were the things that needed to be done. The only people who could do all that were the scientists. And they were all nuts. So, no help there.

Then one day Moriarty showed up at my house.

He looked awful. Like a strung-out drug addict. Which, in a way, he was.

"Punch, I need punch," he said, desperately. He tried to push past me. "Is this where you keep it?"

"Huh?"

"That punch you made for the scientists. It's

all gone, and I never had very much. It's worn off now. I need more."

"Well I don't have any. Try next door."

I started to close the door. He stuck his mouth in it.

"Make some more then. As Mayor of this city, I command you!"

"You're not the Mayor. The Blob is."

"I don't need very much," he wheedled. "Just make me a little bit. It doesn't even have to be exactly the same. It could even be the exact opposite, I don't care, as long as it's punch."

That's when I got my grand idea. The "exact opposite", I thought, as I slammed the door in Moriarty's face. It was the solution to everything! This was one of those many times when having a simple uncluttered mind, and watching science fiction movies all the time when you're supposed to be watching something educational, comes in handy. All I had to do was just reverse the polarity! That's the answer to all science-related problems. I don't know why people waste their time trying other things first. Just stupid, I guess. Minds too cluttered with "thoughts". Reversing the polarity of the punch that had made the scientists insane, and then making them drink this "anti-punch", would instantly restore them to sanity. That was obvious to anyone who had ever watched even the worst science fiction movie. Then, once the scientists were sane again, they could fix everything else that needed fixing. I would have done my bit. I could take the rest of the crisis off. Excitedly, I headed for the Convention Center.

I had assumed there would be guards posted outside the Convention Center that I would have to deal with—guards who would want to know why I was in a restricted area with plans in my mind—but after I had beaten up several creatures, including The Beast With Thick Glasses, The Creature Whose Pants Don't Fit, and The Monster Who Could Afford To Lose A Little Weight, I realized I was just beating up ugly people who were waiting for a bus, not monsters. How was I to know? They looked pretty frightening to me. Anyway, I couldn't take any chances.

The Convention Center was a mess. Dust and cobwebs everywhere. Nobody came here anymore now that the scientists had shifted their base of operations to City Hall. A dusty plaque on the wall said: "On This Spot The First Scientist Went Mad". There were no signs of life anywhere except for some derelict laboratory rats in the corner.

"Spare cheese, asshole?" asked one of them.

I brushed past the rats. I didn't have any spare cheese. Not for them anyway. Lazy... good for nothing... I work for my cheese.

I made my way to the punch bowl, rolled up my sleeves, and got started. I began with basic punch mix, then began adding various chemicals to taste, trying to remember as I went along what exactly I had dumped into the mix the first time, then dumping the exact opposite in now. This was harder than I thought. What's the opposite of sulphur? Molasses? That sounds right, but what if it's wrong? I began to realize that it's easy to say "reverse the polarity"—I say it all the time, about everything—but it's harder to do, especially when the pressure is on, and everybody is counting on you. But I pressed on, dumping every opposite-looking thing I could find into the punch.

When I finally got the lemon slices floating the other way I figured maybe it was done. The punch looked reversed to me. I mean, look for yourself. See the lemons? It's done, isn't it? Sure it is. Now to put it to the test.

The first scientist I tried it on was just finishing an experiment when I burst into his lab.

"I've got it!" he said, excitedly. "The cure for the common cold! No more will man suffer from…"

I grabbed him and forced the anti-punch down his throat.

He writhed around for a moment, then the light of madness faded out of his eyes and the bland boring look of science settled over his face.

"What happened?" he asked. "What day of the Convention is this?" Then he recognized me. "Oh, it's you, Burly. Did you find your enemy?"

He was back to normal, all right. Good. I told you this would work. I don't know where people get the idea that science is hard. Just reverse the polarity, stupid. That's what I always do, egghead.

On to the next scientist, who had just discovered the cure for death and taxes. The same virus caused both of them, he said. And that virus was… but we'll never know what it was, because we don't have time. We have to get that punch down his throat. In a few moments I had him back to normal, and we were both shaking hands with each other, and neither one of us could figure out what that equation on his blackboard meant. Finally, we erased it. So, another success.

Soon all the scientists began coming out into the street rubbing their eyes and looking around like people waking up from a wonderful monster-filled dream.

"Oh, my head!" said Doctor Smiley, holding his temples. "What did I drink last month?"

"Never mind what you drank," I told him, severely, "Do you see what you've done? Look around you. We are at the bottom of the sea, and are being ruled by monsters." I pointed at a group of citizens fleeing in terror from a monster, while another monster filmed it and said it was sensational. "And it's all your doing."

"Wow, great," he said, looking around with amazement.

As impressed as they were by all the imaginative things they'd done—they didn't know they had it in them. People had been telling them they were boring for so long they were starting to believe it—the scientists quickly realized that they had to do something about this. This was a debasement of science, if anything was. If anyone ever started handing out Science Licenses they might not get one. So they quickly went to work to correct what they had done.

It was surprisingly easy for them to take

control of the monsters. All they had to do was say: "Sit-t-t-t!" in a commanding tone, and all the monsters instantly, though unhappily, sat down. You could tell what the monsters were thinking. They were thinking this was bullshit. But there was nothing they could do about it. Except sit.

I asked Doctor Smiley how he had gained control over the monsters so easily. I didn't think even I could have done it that fast.

"Well, we weren't sure what to put in the heads of these monsters when we built them," he said. "The movies glossed over that part. I guess it wasn't considered 'entertaining' enough. So we filled their heads up with movie dialogue, party chit-chat, advertising slogans, Hollywood gossip, and anger. But there was still a lot of room left, so we filled up the rest of the space in their heads with dog engrams."

"I see," I said. Though I didn't, of course. What's an engram? It has something to do with dogs, I know that. I'll have to look that up. Anyway, that was his explanation.

The demoralized movie monsters were led back to the Convention Center with leashes around their necks, while everyone cheered and hooted at them and made derogatory remarks that they would have been afraid to make before, and told the monsters to "roll over" and "play dead" and "say 'mama'". And the monsters had to do it.

Then the scientists put their collective minds to the problem of the defective canopy. They had just written "The Defective Canopy" on a sheet of blank paper and underlined it, when the canopy cracked open in several places, and water began to gush in.

Everybody stopped what they were doing and watched in horror as the cracks in the canopy widened and even more water flooded in. I nudged the guy next to me, who was telling somebody where mankind had gone off the rails, and what he was going to do about it when he stopped working at the gas station and started running the world.

"There's another thing you can fix when you take over," I said, pointing up.

"Shit," he said.

Water continued pouring in, in ever-increasing amounts. The city's power stations became flooded and shut down, so everything in the city went dark and the air stopped circulating. And it was starting to get very cold, very quickly. Someone said we were all going to die, it was all over, we didn't have a chance, we were all dead dead dead, and everybody told me to for God's sake shut up.

I didn't want to die so young—I'm only forty. I've got my whole old age in front of me. I didn't want to miss out on false teeth—but I didn't see what I could do about any of this. There wasn't anything I could reverse the polarity on around here. This wasn't the kind of thing I knew how to fix.

Then I noticed that the water pouring in had drenched my copy of the latest Loose Cannon book, which I was carrying in my back pocket—a book I was only half way through reading. This made me angry, and I felt like slugging somebody. Then I realized that that's exactly what Loose Cannon would do in this situation. He wouldn't try to figure anything out. That was for "thinking detectives". He would just go ape. And somehow everything would work out for the best. So that's what I decided to do.

I ran at the gushing water, pinwheeling my fists and roaring. It didn't make any sense, of course, but that just made me angrier. As I ran, I accidentally clipped a number of people with my flying fists, which were getting bigger and smaller (along with the rest of me), as I totally lost control. The people I hit started swinging at me in return, and in the darkness they usually ended up missing me and hitting someone else. Soon everybody was joining in, in what was rapidly becoming a citywide bar fight.

In the course of this fight a number of chairs were thrown through the canopy. I couldn't criticize those who did this because I guess I threw more chairs through the canopy than anybody. All the same, we probably shouldn't have done it. I guess we just weren't thinking. I was just about to suggest that we throw the next chair somewhere else, when the canopy shattered completely and all the water in the world came rushing in.

CHAPTER FOURTEEN

All the residents of Central City stood around holding their breath and looking at each other, appalled. We were certainly in a bad situation now. Worse than the situation we had been in a minute ago. Instead of the water being up to our knees, now it was over our heads. Thousands of feet over our heads. What to do?

Someone suggested, using hand signals, that maybe if all of us drank as much water as we could, maybe make a contest of it, with the winner to get a lifetime supply of water... but I was quickly, via hand signals, shouted down.

We all looked at each other helplessly. We were doomed. And we knew it. And it didn't take long to figure out whose fault it was. It was that guy standing next to us holding his breath. If it weren't for him everything would be perfect—the water would only be up to our knees. We all resumed fighting with each other.

But now the fight was better than ever, thanks to all the water. Every time I slugged someone in the stomach, all the air they were struggling to hold in was blasted out of them in big bubbles. The harder you hit them, the bigger the bubbles. Hitting people under water is more fun than hitting them on land because you get the big bubbles. Very satisfying. Very satisfying indeed. Of course, big bubbles were coming out of me every time I got hit in the stomach too. But that's okay. That's fair. I don't expect there to be any special rules for me just because I started the fight.

So everybody was holding their breath, then getting a lot of it knocked out of them, then desperately holding onto what little air they had left. I didn't know how much longer this could go on, I'm no doctor, but I hoped it would go on forever. Bubble fight. Ha!

Gradually, the size and number of the bubbles started getting smaller, and I noticed everyone's cheeks were bulging out a lot less. It looked like the fight would be over soon, darnit. It looked like the end. I slugged one more guy, then made my peace with my Maker and waited calmly for death, then slugged another guy who was going past, and three more who had their eyes closed and were making their peace with their Maker (I missed one guy who was apparently warned by his Maker in the nick of time. I heard a deep voice saying: "Look out!")

Just when we were sure we were finished—there were no more bubbles coming out of any of us—the State police and the FBI arrived, wearing oxygen tanks with badges on them, and nightsticks that worked underwater.

"You're all under arrest," announced one of the Federal Agents.

"Good," we all said, using up the last of our air to do so.

"You have the right to remain silent. Anything you say can and will be used against you in a court of law. You have the right to speak to an attorney…"

We all made "skip on down" motions with our hands while we were being read our rights, but the police refused to be hurried. They had to go through the proper procedure or they would catch hell back at the station. After we had been read our rights, and carefully handcuffed, and a latecomer had been read his rights, to everyone's irritation, especially since he had more rights than we did, and some of his rights were better than ours, we finally were all transported back up to the surface.

While we were all sitting around a hot stove at the police station, waiting for our thousands of pairs of pants to dry, and trying to cough the seaweed and buried treasure out of our lungs, I asked one of the policemen how they had found us. He said all the bubbles bursting on the surface had given our location away. I was surprised they could see our bubbles from the shore, but he said they could see our bubbles in Denver (though just barely). So Loose Cannon's "going ape" technique had worked after all, just like we all thought it would.

Police tugs and underwater salvage teams made quick work of dredging up the city, getting it back on land, and transporting it back to the center of our State where it belonged.

The authorities who had been standing there all this time tapping their feet, watched as Central City finally came around the corner and was set back down in its original location. Then they demanded to know who the ringleader was. Who had stolen this city? Who was the evil genius responsible for this spectacular crime?

"I am," said Moriarty, proudly. And, though he certainly only deserved partial credit for everything that had happened, we were perfectly happy to let him take the whole thing.

So even though the rest of us appeared to be at least accomplices of some sort in this strange crime, we just ended up being charged with a few minor violations, like "Being Too Wet To Be Fingerprinted" and "Ruining the Shoes of a Police Officer", fined a few dollars, and released. Some of us also got our heads dunked in a water trough for awhile to teach us to have more respect for the law in the future, but I was kind of used to that, didn't mind it at all. In fact, this was my favorite trough. There's a shiny spot at the bottom that looks like it might be a nickel, but I never quite get it when policemen are dunking my head in there, so I don't know if it's really a nickel or not. But I always like taking another crack at it.

Surprisingly, things didn't turn out badly for Moriarty either. In fact, I don't think they could have turned out much better.

As he was being led away in disgrace—but with a triumphant smile and a handcuffed wave for everyone, as if he'd been arrested for winning the Rose Bowl—the perverse American Public suddenly decided that he was their favorite. He was the Criminal of the Century. He was A Thief-In-A-Million. He was their hero. Hurrah for Moriarty, The People's Choice.

Oh, he still had to go on trial for what he had done, all right. The law demanded that. But it was a Ticker Tape Trial down Broadway, with everyone lining the trial route holding up signs that said: "Welcome Home Moriarty" and "You've Stolen Our Hearts!" and "Hurrah For Morry!" And famous astronauts rode in his limousine with him and served as character witnesses. And the Mayor of New York gave him an Honorary Alibi. The verdict when it was all over? Guilty But Innocent, which was a new verdict created by Special Act of Congress, just for this occasion. And was Moriarty happy? Yes, he was.

The public's sudden and inexplicable infatuation with Moriarty was enough to make you sick. I know it made me sick. I tried to explain to everybody that yes, he has style, and yes, he has caught the public's imagination with his daring and unusual crime, but also, yes, he's a God damn thief who should be in jail, not in a parade. They just said to get out of the way so they could see Morry better. I give up. I'm not kidding, I give up. I'll never understand people, not if I live to be 60.

CHAPTER FIFTEEN

So now Professor Moriarty had what he wanted. He was not only considered a master criminal, he was considered the greatest master criminal of the age. Some people even compared him favorably to the original Professor Moriarty, who they now dismissed as a "Victorian twerp". This new Moriarty was better than all previous Moriartys combined. He was "The Man Who Stole Central City". And everyone was amazed.

He did all the talk shows, of course, and everyone wanted to hear his story, and laugh at the joke the show's gagwriters had written for him ("I'm thinking of stealing your city next!"), and then everyone was surprised to find that he could also sing, that he had a surprisingly pleasant baritone voice.

Once I got over my initial frustration (the man was a thief, not a hero. Put him in jail, not on TV), I realized this whole thing could turn out to be good for me, too. Now I had a world class enemy. An enemy to be proud of. His notoriety would rub off on me—make me look good too. I tried to get on to the talk shows with him, maybe we could sit on the couch together next to Merv or whoever, but they wouldn't let me in. Said I wasn't important. I said they'd change their tune when they found out who Professor Moriarty's enemy was. And they agreed they might.

But it turned out I wasn't his enemy anymore. Now that he was so prominent he had attracted the attention of all the big-time detectives, and his new enemy was my old hero, Loose Cannon, Private Eye. I always thought he was a fictional character, like I am, but apparently not. There he was up on stage with Professor Moriarty. They were glad-handing each other, and throwing shadow punches at each other, and playfully calling each other knuckleheads, and praising each others' resourcefulness, and saying things like: "This man... this glorious man..." until it made you want to gag, because it wasn't you up there in the spotlight being slobbered over, it was somebody else. Then Johnny, or whoever, would say: "I understand you've got a song for us, Professor," and Professor Moriarty would say: "I certainly have, Keith, or whoever", and would launch into a song ("The Impossible Dream" or some song like that. Show tunes, mostly). Then everyone would join in in the chorus, with Loose Cannon wading into the audience and beating the shit out of anyone who wasn't singing good enough, which the people who hadn't been beaten up, who still had their shit, found hilarious.

I was disgusted. I angrily threw away all my Loose Cannon books, my Junior Loose Cannon Club Membership Card, my Loose Cannon Coonskin Cap, my "Rat in the Refrigerator" Board Game (no rats in that either), and all the rest of my Loose Cannon merchandise. I didn't want to have anything to do with the man anymore. He was a poacher. Besides, his style really didn't work for me. I had tried it for an entire book and it didn't make me a dime.

To make up for dumping me, Professor Moriarty sent over his kid brother, Wilfred, to be my enemy for awhile, until school started anyway. But Wilfred didn't really know what to do, kept asking me what "diabolical" meant, and if I was planning on opening that can of peanuts anytime soon. And he kept shooting spitwads at me until he was driving me up the wall. Why do kids do that? It drives me up the wall. Then I discovered that a comic book would keep him quiet. So that's okay now. He's in my other office, quiet as a mouse.

I figured when everybody heard the whole story, everything that had happened, I would be a hero too. I had had a lot to do with this adventure in one way or another. I deserved some notoriety too. So I told them that I was the one who was responsible for the scientists going mad, not Moriarty. And who told the scientists about science fiction movies, and helped them make all those crazy monsters? The same guy who threw the first chair through the canopy, that's who.

Me. Frank Burly. Most of this wouldn't have happened if it hadn't been for me, honest.

When I finally got them to believe me, the perverse American Public, instead of worshipping me like it did Moriarty, decided it didn't like me at all. I was a meddler, a bungler. Everything was my fault. I was the public's new whipping boy. Their old whipping boy—a Congressman who had said that secret love nests were good for the economy—sent me a thank-you card for getting him off the front page. Nice of him, but it didn't get the perverse American Public off my back.

Since I was responsible for all the bad things that had happened, they made me clean it all up. I had to nail the city back into place by myself, bail a lot of water out, and do all sorts of cleaning projects nobody else wanted to do. How do you get Frankenstein crap off a car windshield? Anybody know how to do that? Because everything I use just makes it smear worse.

The monsters came out of this all right. When the cops grabbed us, the monsters—who were trained actors, after all—quickly put on dorky looking clothes and pretended to be just ordinary ugly citizens, instead of the imprisoned supernatural creatures they really were, and were released with the rest of us. Last I heard, they had formed a repertory company and were touring the country doing plays in their "Karloff In The Park" series, to small, but baffled, audiences. So they're doing okay. They're comfortable.

The scientists came out of all this all right,

too. They sold one of their seemingly unusable early experiments, a modified lab rabbit who could play all nine positions on a baseball field at once, and could win the game all by himself, to the New York Yankees, making enough in the deal to pay for a new research laboratory, which they are using to figure out how I made that punch. So I guess if this were their story it would be a happy ending. But it's my story, darnit.

Things turned out kind of lousy for me. On top of everything else, I seem to be permanently fifty feet tall now. I was changing around a lot there for awhile, usually when it was most inconvenient, like my ass would get really big just when the police were about to kick it, or my head would get really small when I was asking someone for a date. Finally I tried to fix it by giving the side of my head an extra hard whack. Well, I fixed it all right. I stopped changing, but not until I cycled through every possible size and shape combination, before finally settling on the size I am now. And no amount of whacks will get me to change again. So now I seem to be stuck at fifty feet tall for the rest of my amazing colossal life.

The furniture company won't deliver any more furniture to me—they said they've had enough. They're going out of business, and joining the Coast Guard—so I'm stuck with the last batch they sent, which is for a two inch tall, ten foot wide detective, with eyeballs the size of freight cars. It's all the wrong size for me, but it looks like I'm going to have to learn to live with it. I've found that I can balance on the biggest armchair if I'm careful, and make sure not to breathe in or out. If you know of a way to solve my furniture problem, let me know. You can tell me about it when I'm looking down your chimney.